"Are you sure about us, Adrian? I mean, is this what you really want? I want you with me, but it scares me."

"And the thought of my not being with you scares me, Caprice. You're not alone anymore, sweetheart."

"You want me," she whispered, more as a reassurance to herself than as a statement or question. Sometimes she still didn't believe this was happening to her. Couldn't believe how lucky she was to have Adrian in her life, in her heart. And her in his. He always knew what to say, what to do to make her feel better. Make her feel safe. Make her feel loved.

They traded one passionate kiss, followed by a brief one, and then jumped up together and ran after the children. It could be a good life, Caprice thought—a life with someone who understood her, who supported her, who shared her passions. Someone who loved both her and Isabella. Someone she loved with all her heart. And a little boy she now loved, too.

Yes, it would be a very good life.

Dear Reader,

I'm still amazed that I'm allowed to write these touching stories. When you consider the kinds of books we've been privileged to read from Harlequin throughout the years, and the awesome authors brought to us—some of the greatest authors in the world—it makes you stop and think just how much Harlequin romances have influenced our lives.

The first time I was affected by Harlequin, I was barely a teenager, looking for something suitable for the reading needs of a starry-eyed teen. I found a book about two extraordinary people trying to save a ranch. I'd never read a book set in such an exciting place, and I must admit I was hooked. That book opened so many reading doors for me and increased my desire to expand my reading.

I never dreamt that I would actually write for Harlequin, but when that opportunity arose I wanted to bring some of the excitement of falling in love and the happily ever after I've always counted on in Harlequin romances to my own readers. Maybe even to that dreamy-eyed teenager who's on the verge of falling in love. I am so grateful to be able to write these stories, and I'd like to extend my deepest thanks to Harlequin for allowing me to do so.

Wishing you health and happiness, and the most beautiful happily ever after in your own life!

Dianne Drake

P.S.—I love hearing from you, so please feel free to e-mail me at Dianne@DianneDrake.com, or visit my Web site at www.DianneDrake.com.

A FAMILY FOR THE CHILDREN'S DOCTOR
Dianne Drake

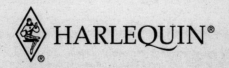

TORONTO • NEW YORK • LONDON
AMSTERDAM • PARIS • SYDNEY • HAMBURG
STOCKHOLM • ATHENS • TOKYO • MILAN • MADRID
PRAGUE • WARSAW • BUDAPEST • AUCKLAND

ISBN-13: 978-0-373-19905-1
ISBN-10:   0-373-19905-8

A FAMILY FOR THE CHILDREN'S DOCTOR

First North American Publication 2008

www.eHarlequin.com

Printed in U.S.A.

A FAMILY FOR THE CHILDREN'S DOCTOR

CHAPTER ONE

IT WAS beautiful land down there. So lush and green. Trees as far as the eye could see. It had a certain peaceful quality to it he liked. Peaceful…hopeful…something he needed in his life.

Dr Adrian McCallan stared down over the treetops in the jungle below, excited by the prospect of what lay ahead of him, yet dreading the two weeks it would take to accomplish his promise. He wanted to be here. Had wanted it for a very long time now. Yet he didn't, and that little bit of dread in him was using up all the peacefulness he had in reserve. Until now, he'd truly never known what it felt like to be ripped in half.

Now he did.

Physically he was here, ready to do the work. Intellectually he was intact and up to the chore. But emotionally he was far away. He shut his eyes, conjuring up an image of what he was leaving behind and, as always, the face that he envisioned brought a sure smile to his face. It always did.

In a sense, it was amazing that he was going through all these conflicting feelings. That he *could* go through all these feelings. It hadn't been that long ago that feeling *anything* had been foreign to him. It wasn't that he hadn't been able to, but more that he hadn't wanted to. It had made life easier that way, without encumbrances. But now he had a personal testimony to what they said—absence *did* make the heart grow fonder. Absolutely! Or, in his case, tore it into shreds. For him, the pain of absence was almost a physical one, and he was glad to feel it. Glad for the reason to feel it.

Yet what he was about to do—working with all those children—he'd wanted to do this, wanted to get involved in something so worthy for a long time now. That part of the absence he didn't regret in the least. But the other part…

Sighing, he opened his eyes and stared out the window again, listening to the low drone of the airplane engines. The rumble of the monotone these last two hours should have dulled his senses, but all it had done had been to give him empty time in which to doubt his choice to come here. He'd known it was going to be tough being away from Sean, but he hadn't counted on it being this tough, and so early on. For God's sake, he was only into it a day and already it felt like a week…a month…a year. Which was ridiculous. But damn it! He already missed his son. Separated from the person he loved most in this world by only twenty-four hours and already he missed him like hell.

What in the world was he going to be like being away from him for a full two weeks?

That he didn't even want to think about. One day at a time. That's what he was promising himself. He'd get through it one day at a time and each day spent would mean one day closer to Sean.

Still, with all the internal reassurances that he could do this, and with his son's own stamp of approval that his daddy was going away to do a very good thing, he couldn't fight his mixed emotions. Operation Smiling Faces was such a worthy cause. Dr Caprice Bonaventura and her group provided valuable medical services to children who might not otherwise receive the help they needed. He'd read about her in a journal a while ago, then listened to her speak at a medical seminar well over a year ago. After that he'd finally made the decision to add his name to her volunteer roster, but only as an anesthesiologist on an emergency basis, as he did have Sean to consider. Two weeks at a time was what Dr Bonaventura asked of her volunteers, and that's what he'd agree to do—once, maybe twice a year. It wasn't much in terms of what other volunteers gave but, at this point in his life, it was all he had. In Sean's life, two weeks was for ever, although he did understand why his father was leaving for a little while. *To help other children.* Sean had been good with that, and very mature for a six-year-old.

More mature than he himself actually, as right now he wasn't sure he had two weeks in him to give. Not with the way he was missing his son.

"Can I get you anything?" the flight attendant asked him. "Water? Maybe a cola or a packet of peanuts? Something to settle your stomach?"

"It shows?" Adrian asked.

She laughed. "I recognize that expression on your face. See it all the time. A little airsickness."

Not airsickness. This wasn't anything that could be cured with a little bromo or Dramamine. "No, thank you," he said, recognizing the edge in his voice. "I'm fine for now," he continued, forcing himself to sound a little less wound up. "But you'll be the first one to know if I do need something." He forced a smile at her. Not a convincing one, but apparently she didn't notice that, because the smile she returned was genuine.

"You just do that," the attendant said, then bounced away to tend to a little old lady who was in a fit to have one of those tiny, overpriced bottles of booze. Scotch, she was demanding over the buzzing voices of the other passengers.

Scotch…if he were a drinking man he might just have one himself. Except he didn't drink. And if he did, drowning his feelings in alcohol wouldn't blot them out. More like just make them sloppy, thinking how this was the first time in six years he'd been separated from Sean for more than a couple of days, thinking how he was feeling damned guilty over it. Not that his son really cared so much. Two weeks with his grandmother was an adventure any six-year-old loved. And Sean would exploit that in every way someone his age could with an over-indulgent granny. Trips to the park, the zoo, to the toy store, to buy ice cream… Knowing that his own mother would take care of Sean did make him feel better. But not enough.

Adrian smiled, thinking about Sean's big plans. Big boy at age six. Bright. The single most abiding love of Adrian's life and the person who made him the happiest.

The one person who defined his life.

Adrian sighed again, closing his eyes to think about his red-headed, green-eyed ball of energy. Two weeks was an awfully long time to be separated from him, and while he still didn't regret his decision to volunteer with Operation Smiling Faces, he did wish there was a way to have the best of both worlds—his son *and* this volunteer job. Caprice Bonaventura did allow children along. But the court had been specific in the child custody decree, thanks to his ex-wife Sylvie's selfish motives. She didn't care about Sean. All she cared about was herself, and the child support payments. Somewhere in her tiny little brain she'd fixed a notion that if Adrian took Sean traveling it could mean he wouldn't bring him back, which might also mean no more money for Sylvie. Of course, that wasn't the case. Miami was home and stability for Sean, and apparently Adrian was the only one concerned with that.

Nevertheless, the judge had ordered restricted travel for Sean as part of Adrian's joint custody with Sylvie, and any travel across the border came only with court approval, which couldn't happen in two days, as that was all the notice Adrian had received for this emergency trip to Costa Rica.

So Sylvie, who never saw Sean unless it benefitted her in some way, had won again and Adrian and Sean were separated now because of her. Not that she cared. But on the bright side, Sean was having the time of his life with his grandmother, safe and sound, and there was nothing Sylvie could do to ruin that.

Damn that Sylvie, anyway. Why did she always find a way to mess up their lives?

"The pilot has instructed the passengers to buckle up for the final approach," the flight attendant said, shaking Adrian out of his thoughts. He opened his eyes to find her bending over him, her big brown eyes fixed on his face, her smile at him so bright it nearly blinded him. She was so close he could smell the faint trace of her flowery perfume in his nostrils. She was a good-looking woman, not that it mattered. Once upon a time he might have shown some interest in the sexuality she was obviously putting on display for him. But not any more. Not for a very long time. Seven years, to be exact. Oh, he'd enjoyed occasional dates, but nothing more than once or twice as his spare time belonged to his son. "He says the landing could be a little rough." She deliberately picked up the seat belt that was dangling over the edge of his seat and dropped it into his lap. "Wouldn't want you getting hurt."

Rough landing, rough heart. Nothing a seat belt could take care of. "Thank you," he said. "I appreciate the warning," he added quickly, still forcing himself to sound nicer than he felt.

"We aim to please," she replied, with a genuinely kind smile and eyes that widened in a bit of hope. He recognized the look. He'd seen it before, not that it ever did any good when it was directed at him.

Encouraged by this, the flight attendant lingered over him a little longer than she should have, giving him ample opportunity to whisper something to her. *An invitation to dinner, an invitation to bed...* But when he didn't, she straightened back up, blushing from the conspicuous rejection, and scurried away to hide in the service cubby where drinks and snacks were prepared.

* *'*

You could have had her, the blue-haired, tattooed young man sitting across the aisle from Adrian said. Actually, he didn't say the words aloud, but the look on the kid's face spoke volumes. And the kid was right. He probably could have had her. Or any number of women he'd encountered over the past few years. But there wasn't extra time in his life, and given his choice between spending time with them and being with Sean…well, there was no contest.

Hard choice sometimes. But a good one always. He didn't regret it.

On principle, he didn't regret his choice to come to Costa Rica either, and he wasn't about to bow out of his responsibility. He wanted to do this, actually—to work with the children. Especially since he'd turned his anesthesiology practice into pediatric anesthesiology, but now that he was on his way, and missing his son like he was, he was having second thoughts.

Adrian smiled. It was crazy, worrying about Sean, who was having the time of his life. That's what Adrian had to remember. And it did comfort him some when he did, even though a little residual wistfulness for something more in his life did flash by. A relationship? A wife? He didn't rule them out for his future, but after his first time through with Sylvie, he didn't rule them in either. Too many complications, he thought as he turned to stare out the window while they started to descend.

If there was one thing he and Sean didn't need, it was any more complications. Over the years, that had become a mantra of sorts.

Below, as the plane swept ever closer to the ground, he saw a banana plantation and all he could think of was how much Sean loved bananas. Of course, Sean's granny would give him bananas. Knowing that, however, didn't make easier the anguish of missing his son, or the emptiness he was feeling.

* * *

"But I don't want to read another book!" Isabella Bonaventura was being stubborn just now. Caprice knew it, and indulged it, as her daughter jerked her hand away from her mother's and plopped down in a black fake leather chair, her back to the windows overlooking the runway. "And I don't want to draw pictures or write another story." She folded her arms irritably across her chest and pulled her face into an angry frown, huffing out a melodramatic sigh. "I'm bored. I want to go back to the hospital."

The hospital, meaning home. They were staying in one of the visitors' suites at the Golfo Dulce Hospital just outside Golfito—a strikingly beautiful area with modern amenities. Many children were coming in which apparently kept Isabella better occupied than *she* was doing today. Poor child was bored out of her mind, waiting, and Caprice couldn't blame her. So was she! "We'll go as soon as he gets here," Caprice replied for the tenth time in twenty minutes.

"How much longer will th-that be?" Isabella shifted in her seat to look out to the runway. "I don't see any planes landing."

Caprice glanced at her watch. The plane was already over thirty minutes late, which, loosely translated into kiddie hours, was about a lifetime. Or so it seemed, anyway, to both child and mother. "Should be any minute," she said, keeping her fingers crossed that would be the case.

Any number of the Operation Smiling Faces crew had volunteered to watch Isabella. So had Josefina, Isabella's Costa Rican caregiver. Caprice had refused the offers, though, and now she was beginning to think she should have taken somebody up on one of them. But she spent so much time away from her daughter as it was, she simply didn't want to be separated from her. Of course, Isabella had an opinion in the matter, too, and hers was not anything like Caprice's.

But in a sense Isabella's mood was to be expected. Yesterday, her eighth birthday, hadn't been a good day either. Caprice knew these few days were going to be rough. Birthday time and holidays were always when Isabella's father forgot her. Which he always did.

"Can I get something to d-drink?"

"You just finished a guava juice," Caprice said, her patience stretching out to a most tenuous thread.

Isabella regarded the empty bottle, made an annoyed face, then looked back at her mother. "I wanted fresco de maracuyá," she said, forming the words with deliberate care.

Passionfruit. A local favorite, and right about now that sounded good to Caprice, too. What sounded better, though, was hearing Isabella attempt the language. "But they don't have that here, sweetie," she said, knowing that wouldn't make any difference. Isabella was tired, bored, impatient and nothing short of a miracle was going to change her mood. Except, perhaps, a mother's best bribe. Caprice smiled. "The plane will be here in just a few minutes, then we'll be going. We'll stop for ice cream on the way back to meet Grant." Dr Etana "Grant" Makela, her resident GP and short-hop pilot.

"Ith cream?" Isabella said, suddenly forgetting her mood now that something had caught her interest.

"Say it properly," Caprice instructed.

"Ith…ice cream." Getting the words out was an effort, but when she had, Isabella looked pleased with herself.

Sometimes it was still a struggle, but most of the time her daughter was able to work through her speech difficulties, thanks to a great speech therapist back home. And thanks to Isabella herself, who was determined to get it right and go beyond anything expected of her. She worked harder than any child should ever have to, and sometimes Caprice feared all the struggles and work would deprive Isabella of her childhood. It was a difficult balance, keeping everything in its proper perspective. But so far Isabella seemed fine with the rigors and the balance.

Her daughter still had a little trouble with some of her words, especially when she was tired or excited. Overall, though, the difference was nothing short of a miracle. From a little girl who had shied away from people and never spoken to the Isabella who existed right now. A miracle of grand proportions and Caprice's inspiration for these trips to Costa Rica.

She was grateful the therapist had released Isabella to come along to Costa Rica for a month. She'd traveled with her before, but only for short trips. Two weeks at the most. And Isabella didn't always come along on some of those shorter trips because of school commitments. But on this, the timing was perfect. School was out on holiday. One thing Caprice would never do was interrupt her daughter's regular routine, but this trip was interrupting nothing except several weeks of play, which she could do as well in Costa Rica as she could in California. And she seemed to have more friends here. So it couldn't have worked out better. *Except for Isabella's birthday, that was.* The residual mood from that was spilling over into this debacle of a trip to the airport, since Isabella was usually much more cheery than she was being now.

"Vanilla ice cream," Caprice said, knowing what came next.

"Chocolate. I want chocolate!"

"But I thought you liked vanilla best."

"You like vanilla best, silly," Isabella squealed, her dark mood finally lightening.

"But I thought I was the one who liked chocolate, *silly.*"

"No, you don't. I do!"

"Are you sure?" Caprice asked, laughing.

"Are *you* sure?" Isabella retorted, laughing, too. They played word games, light banter back and forth as practice exercises. Caprice guided Isabella through the difficult words and as they were having fun and Isabella relaxed she always, without fail, got them right. A year ago, Isabella had barely spoken. Two years ago, she never did unless she'd had to. Now there was no stopping her.

Damn that Tony, Caprice thought, as the light-hearted mother-daughter banter continued for the next few minutes. He threw away the best child in the whole world because she embarrassed him. All because she'd been born with a cleft lip and palate.

She thought back to the day of Isabella's birth. The excitement, the expectation during all those months of pregnancy—she hadn't wanted to know if it was a boy or girl. She'd wanted to be surprised. Then all she'd seen after she'd heard the doctor say it was a girl had been a beautiful daughter. All Tony had seen had been a facial deformity.

His loss, the idiot. "We'll both have chocolate," Caprice said, pulling her daughter into her arms for a hug. Tony's loss, her gain. And such a wonderful one.

"Dr Bonaventura?"

Startled, Caprice looked up from her embrace to the man towering over her. Then she blinked. He was…not what she expected. For some strange reason she'd had elderly fixed in her mind. Along with that image went gray-haired, little wire-rimmed glasses slipping down to the end of his nose, wrinkles. If *this* was the Dr Adrian McCallan, who'd signed on for two weeks, she'd certainly been wrong.

Caprice straightened up, then stood to greet him. "Dr McCallan?" she asked, surprised by the tightness of her voice. Oh, she'd talked to him on the phone once—cellphone, bad connection, crackly voice. With their combined hectic schedules, they'd mostly e-mailed.

Then there was the matter of his résumé. Accolades all over the place, all that seemed to indicate…well, someone much older than what she was seeing. Director of a large medical practice, head anesthesiologist over thirteen others. Part-time med school professor. Well published in medical journals. Noted lecturer. No wonder she'd expected seventy and tired. But the man extending his hand to hers was half that age and…well, it wasn't exactly a tired look she saw on him, but it was one she couldn't quite define.

Next time she was going to request a photo with the résumé.

"It's good to meet you, Dr McCallan, and I'm grateful you could do this on such short notice. Monica Gilbert, who was set to come out as anesthesiologist, had a pregnancy complication, and I'm so happy to get you at the last minute. Especially someone who specializes in pediatrics. It's not every day we have a pediatric anesthesiologist join us, and…"

Was she really babbling at him? It certainly sounded that way. Babbling, giddy like a schoolgirl… He already knew the facts, didn't need a recap. "And thank you." She clamped her mouth shut before any other foolishness slipped out.

"My pleasure," he said, his eyes darting briefly to Isabella, pausing for a moment, then returning his focus to her. "I've been looking forward to doing this for quite some time and, as it happens, the timing worked out." He glanced back at Isabella.

Caprice's first reaction was to bristle. She always did. Call her over-protective, call her over-reactive, and that was fine. She was. But so many people had stared at Isabella before all the corrective surgeries and been horribly cruel to her daughter that her natural tendency was to protect her. And to get riled when someone stared. She knew she was often over the top with her reactions, but that still didn't stop her. Any mother would have done the same.

Instinctively, Caprice stepped in front of Isabella to shield her from Dr McCallan's stare. Although he wasn't exactly staring. It was more like he was trying to make eye contact with a child who still rarely ever did. "We have a long flight ahead of us," she said stiffly. "I think we'd best be going if we want to get to Dulce by nightfall." Dulce, the nickname for the hospital.

Isabella peeked out from behind her mother. "Ith…ice

cream?" she asked, forming deliberate words as she stared at Adrian's kneecaps.

Caprice didn't want to disappoint her daughter, but she also didn't want to have ice cream with this man. He made her uncomfortable. Because of Isabella, perhaps. Or maybe because he was half the age she'd expected and gorgeous in a way she simply didn't want to acknowledge. Whatever the reason, she was ill at ease, and glad the normal seven-hour trip by road would be greatly reduced when they took to the air.

"Maybe another time," she said to Isabella. "I'm sure Dr McCallan is tired from his long trip, and anxious to get settled in."

"I like ice cream," Adrian said, twisting his head to see Isabella, who finally met his gaze with a cautious gaze of her own and the tiniest little smile tugging at the corners of her mouth. "Vanilla. What kind do you like?" he asked her.

"Vanilla," she said, taking one step away from her mother. "Just like you. It's my favorite."

"Then I think we should have vanilla." He glanced up at Caprice. "If that's OK with your mother."

"She likes chocolate," Caprice said, almost sounding adamant about it. Her daughter was already smitten with this man... smitten enough to change her favorite ice cream flavor for him. It stung some, having Isabella's attention, and possibly affections, divided just a little. It was only momentary, she knew, but that didn't lessen the feeling that Isabella was so eager to allow someone else in. It had been just the two of them for so long she'd never thought in terms of anybody else. *Especially not a man.*

Caprice shut her eyes and drew in a deep breath, willing her sensibility back. Dr McCallan wasn't a threat. He was merely Isabella's reaction after another disappointment, courtesy of her father. That's all. "Chocolate," she whispered, trying to focus on something other than the man standing mere inches away. "We both like chocolate."

"I like what he likes," Isabella protested. "Va-vanilla!"

Adrian squatted down. "And you are?"

"Itha…Ith…Is-a-bella!"

"And I'm Adrian, Isabella." He extended his hand to her, and she was not at all hesitant to take it. In fact, Caprice thought Isabella clung a little too long to Adrian's hand. Another after-effect of another disappointment from her father, she supposed. Isabella didn't often have a man in her life and Adrian cut an imposing figure to an eight-year-old, as well as to a thirty-four-year-old. Tall, chestnut-colored hair, brown eyes. Friendly brown eyes, the kind that would smile even when his mouth didn't. And nice, broad shoulders… She almost caught herself sighing over his broad shoulders. But she didn't, of course. Instead, she took Isabella by the hand and led her down the corridor in the airport terminal, leaving Adrian to follow along behind them.

It was an odd first meeting. More than she expected, and a whole lot less. Not that she was sure what that meant. But Adrian McCallan wasn't the stodgy old codger she'd thought him to be. Which could be a powerful problem, as it seemed her young daughter was already in full-fledged infatuation, dragging her heels, looking back at him and flirting in the way only an eight-year-old girl could flirt. "You're getting chocolate," Caprice said. "And that's final!"

"So what brings you out here?" Adrian asked, taking a seat across from Caprice and Isabella in a little sweet shop in downtown San José. Already Isabella had chocolate smeared on her face, and instinctively he handed her his napkin. "Other than the surgeries you do, why Costa Rica?"

"This was the first place I ever came with Operation Smiling Faces and I fell in love with it."

She had a little speck of chocolate above her lip and he handed her a napkin, too. Caprice Bonaventura…everything he'd expected in a good surgeon, and so much more. He'd known she was beautiful, even though he'd only seen her from afar. Then when he'd read the article about her, he'd been amazed by the scope of her work. Plastic surgery got such a bad rap. Vanity medicine was what most people thought. A new nose, eyelid readjustment, breast implants. That came to mind right off when you thought of a plastic surgeon. But she didn't do vanity work. It was all corrective—birth defects, accidents, severe illness. She was an amazing doctor in the field. Noted internationally for her work. And up close, even the word "beautiful" seemed lacking. Caprice was exquisite. Shoulder-length black hair pulled back to the nape of her neck in a no-nonsense style, which made her look sexy as hell. Dark brown eyes surrounded by thick, black eyelashes. Sexy as hell again. And her body… No man should be having those kinds of thoughts about a woman with the woman's daughter sitting next to her. But, damn it, Caprice was enough to rob a man of his breath, then hold it for ransom.

And that wasn't just his long stretch of abstinence talking.

Sexy aside, though, she was a little tight where her daughter was concerned. Over-protective didn't go far enough in describing what he was seeing right here. Isabella was a bright, outgoing child, beautiful like her mother, but Caprice seemed to stifle all that in her, and if there was one thing he did not want in his life, it was a woman with issues. Mother issues, professional issues, relationship issues. Issues of any kind. He'd had one, and Sylvie's had been just the opposite of Caprice's… She didn't want to mother her child at all… Issues were issues. He steered clear. And that was going to include the over-stressed mother sitting across from him now. Which, admittedly, took away from some of that sexy-as-hell aura she'd been exuding.

No, he didn't go anywhere near a woman like her. Burned once, and he wasn't going back to the flame. Not even anywhere near it. That was his motto as well as his sworn oath.

"So you've kept coming back?" he asked, deliberately staring at his ice cream rather than at Caprice lest his motto wanted to slip a little.

"I know the area, the people. And as far as I'm concerned, Costa Rica is the most beautiful place on earth. As long as the children here need my help, this is where I'll keep coming back."

"And you've done how many surgeries?"

"Just over one hundred fifty now."

"All free of charge?"

Caprice nodded. "It's not about the money. We have sources who fund us, especially after they see the smiles." She herself smiled, talking about her work. "And, like you, our staff is all volunteers."

"It's worthy," Adrian commented, just as his cellphone jingled.

"You'll have to go outside to get reception," Caprice said. "And once we're out in the jungle, you won't get any at all. It's back to the old-fashioned land lines."

He glanced down at the number. His mother's. Probably Sean wanting to talk to him, and as this might be the last time for a while, he was glad to step outside to say his temporary goodbyes to his son.

"Sylvie took him," were his mother's first words, after Adrian answered.

"What do you mean, Sylvie took him?" he said, not yet alarmed.

"She came by earlier, and demanded to take Sean out for ice cream."

"You let her?"

"She has shared custody, Adrian. I couldn't stop her, could I?"

Damn, he hated shared custody. He'd fought for more at the original hearing and lost as the judge had believed a mother had rights, too. Under most circumstances Adrian would have agreed. But not in this case. Not with Sean. "So she hasn't brought him back?" The warning hairs on the back of his neck were beginning to stand up.

"Not yet."

"How long?" he asked, trying hard not to sound irritated with his mother. It wasn't her fault after all. It was Sylvie's.

"Five hours, Adrian." Emma McCallan began to sniffle. "I'm sorry. I didn't want to let him go with her, but she had papers... court papers."

The infamous custody agreement. She always used it when she wanted something from him...money, mostly. "Did she tell you which ice-cream parlor?"

"Yes, and I called them. Sylvie and Sean haven't been there."

"And you tried calling her house?"

"Phone's been disconnected."

Now the warning hairs on his neck were rioting.

"Have you called Ben?" Benjamin Rafferty, his attorney.

"Yes, and he's reported it to the police, but the police said that since Sylvie does have partial custody there's nothing they can do about it if the child's not in danger."

"She runs off with my son and there's nothing they can do?" He glanced back in the window at Caprice, who was staring at him, then turned his back to her. "Have him call a private investigator."

"What if she hurts Sean?"

"She won't. This is just for effect." Sylvie was a lot of things, most of them not so nice, but she would never hurt her son. She wasn't cruel like that at all, and as much as he wanted to throttle her for doing this, he truly didn't fear for Sean's safety. Not physical safety, anyway. But his emotional well-being...that was something entirely different. "She asked me to up her child support payments last week. Up them permanently. Enough to nearly wipe me out, and I turned her down." He'd given in every single time before when she'd come at him, each time against his attorney's advice. After all, Sylvie didn't have custodial care of Sean, just occasional visitation rights, which legally entitled her to no financial support. But he'd done it merely to make things easier, to avoid arguments. To protect Sean.

In fact, if anything, she was legally obligated to pay Adrian child support. Which she didn't, and he wouldn't have accepted had she offered. But what she did was demand it from him in large amounts, always with the threat of dragging their whole custody issue into court one more time, which would pull Sean right into the middle of it. And Sean didn't need to be part of the ugliness between his parents.

Adrian would not allow that. Not under any circumstances. It had already happened at the initial hearings after they'd separated, and Sean had suffered. So, not again. It was easier to meet the woman's demands and leave his son out of it altogether. Except the last demand had been unreasonable. She'd wanted practically every penny he had, and in one lump sum at that!

That's where he'd drawn the line and, for the first time in their rocky relationship, said no! Now Sylvie was having her say in the matter. "Tell Ben to get me the best he can find, and that I'll be on the first plane back to Miami."

"What about your obligations there in Costa Rica?" his mother asked.

What about them? He turned back around and saw Caprice still staring at him. "I'll find someone else to take my place." Though he knew that was easier said than done. He was the replacement. Replacing the replacement wasn't going to be easy. Not on such short notice. He'd had to move heaven and earth to set his schedule aside for this, and getting someone else to do the same… "I'll be home as soon as I can. And if Sylvie does bring Sean back, don't let her near him again, Mom, no matter what kind of papers she shows you. Promise me you won't let her near him until I'm there and can deal with her face to face."

As he clicked off the phone and jammed it back in his pocket, he hesitated for a moment, trying to gather his wits before going back into the ice-cream parlor and walking over to the table where mother and daughter were finishing off their ice creams.

It wasn't fair to leave them in the lurch here, but he needed to be back home for Sean. His son came first. That's all there was to it. "Dr Bonaventura," he said before he'd even stopped in front of them, "I'm afraid I've got some bad news for you."

CHAPTER TWO

BAD news. Why wasn't she surprised? Judging from his body language throughout his phone call, she'd been pretty sure the news wasn't good. Then, when he'd caught her eye and deliberately turned his back, she'd gotten the distinct impression that his bad news, in some way, affected her. Which could only mean he was backing out of his promise. The expression on his face right now confirmed it.

Caprice braced herself for the actual words, still hoping she was wrong. "Why do I get the feeling your bad news has direct bearing on me and Operation Smiling Faces?"

"Because it does. I have to return to Miami as soon as I can catch a plane out of here. Family emergency."

"Someone died?" she gasped.

Adrian shook his head.

"Injured, ill?"

He shook his head again.

Now she was beginning to wonder. "Disaster?"

"No. Just something personal I need to take care of."

Personal? The man had a personal problem and he was about to dump them? She shook her head in disbelief. It truly hadn't crossed her mind that someone with such a sterling reputation as Adrian McCallan's would back out on her. But he was doing just that, and he wasn't giving her a good reason. There were many things she could and would accept, but a vague personal reason? "And what about your obligation here?" she asked, trying to delay her anger in case there really was a valid reason for him leaving.

"I don't have a choice. I've been called back because of…" He frowned. "It's complicated. Let's just say that some finished business back home wasn't as finished as I'd thought it was."

"Unfinished business." Initial shock over with now, it was all beginning to sink in and the anger was starting to bubble. He was leaving for nothing that seemed all that pressing, which meant there would be a shortage in her medical teams. They were geared up for four teams, and Adrian's departure would reduce their workforce by one-fourth, because without the anesthesiologist the surgeon could not operate. As simple as that. Children expecting follow-up surgeries, or even the beginning surgeries in a long series of procedures, wouldn't get what they expected because of Adrian's *unfinished business*. In his two weeks here, that could mean as many as fifteen or twenty surgeries not getting done, fifteen or twenty children expecting a miracle and a smile being turned away. More tears over more ridicule.

"I don't suppose you'd like to tell me what this unfinished business is, would you? I have numerous contacts back in the States, and maybe I can find someone to take care of your problems so you won't have to leave." Nice try, but from the dead hard set to his face, she knew she'd failed. He wasn't about to tell her any more than he already had.

"Nothing you can help with," he said gruffly. "And I'm sorry it worked out this way. I really intended to fulfill my part of the obligation. Unfortunately, it's simply not meant to be this time."

"Not meant to be?" she exploded, unable to keep it in any longer. "You're pushing this off like it's a casual trip to the grocery store. Can't go this time but maybe next time. I resent that, Doctor, since so many people are depending on you as part of the surgical team." Caprice glanced at Isabella, who'd stopped eating and was staring up wide-eyed at her, then she took a deep breath to steady herself. "We had an agreement, Dr McCallan," she said stiffly, aware that there was no way, legal or otherwise, she could keep him there if he chose to leave. "I counted on you keeping your word."

"So did I, Dr Bonaventura, but, like I said, something came up."

"So, what am I supposed to do? Tell my patients that they'll have to go away because *something came up*? Try to schedule them for another time, even though my next three trips down here are already booked solid with former patients? Tell them, tough luck, that a hemangioma doesn't matter, or that Goldenhar syndrome can be fixed by heavy cosmetics, low-brimmed hats and lots of scarves? Because that's not good enough. These people expect that when I promise them a procedure I'll deliver it, and part of that delivery is you, Dr McCallan. Some of these children have waited for years and it's not fair to tell them I'll have to put them back on the list, that they might have to wait another few months or years." She slapped her napkin down on the table, scooted her chair back across the floor so hard it hit the empty chair behind her, and stood. "That's not good enough. And it's not fair."

"I'll find a replacement," he offered. "As soon as I return I'll make some calls."

"And have someone here when? By tomorrow morning? Because that's when we open the clinic and start evaluating patients, looking at new cases coming in—*and there will be dozens of them*—and doing physicals for the children already scheduled for surgery. Will you have me that replacement by then, Doctor?"

"Who's next on the list?" he asked. "I'll call them right now, and I'll assume the financially responsibility to get them here. I mean, it's really not my intention to cause you any problems here. So, I'll be glad to—"

"You're next on the list, Doctor," Caprice interrupted. "My other replacement wasn't available, and the one after that is out with another of the Operation Smiling Face units right now. Meaning you were last on the list."

"Last on the list?" he sputtered.

"Last. *Very last.* People are good to send money, but finding time to volunteer is another thing."

"He's not coming back to Dulce with us?" Isabella piped up.

Caprice turned to her daughter, fighting hard to erase the angry expression from her face. "No, sweetie, he's not. He's got to go back home as soon as he can."

Isabella scrunched her face into a sulky little frown, then crossed her arms angrily across her chest. "I don't want him to. I want Adrian to stay."

Great, just great! One fleeing doctor, one pouting child. Could this day get any worse? "So do I, but it's not my decision to make."

"But you're the boss," she cried. "Can't you make him?"

Caprice turned back to Adrian. "What would it take to convince you to stay?" she asked, the anger returning the instant she looked at him. This man was really leaving her in a lurch, and all she could think about were the disappointments and heartbreak she would have to cause. She hated that. Hated him for being the cause of it. "If it's money—"

"Not money," he interrupted. "Like I said, it's just some matters that need my attention."

"Can't they wait for two weeks?"

He shook his head. "Look, I feel bad about this. I really wanted to come out here and do the work. And I'll be willing to come back at another time…"

"Once is all you get, Doctor. I can't afford second chances when somebody stands me up on the first chance. Not with the workload we carry here. It would be foolish of me to trust you again. Wouldn't you agree?"

"Then maybe one of the other units will have me in the future because I really want to do this. But right now I've got to get home. Sorry about that."

Sorry? He was sorry? "Not half as sorry as the children will be," she said, taking Isabella by the hand and leading her away from the table. As Caprice swished by Adrian, she shoved the check for the ice cream at him, then marched on out the door. Wasn't much of a last word, and ever since her marriage to Tony had ended, she tried always to get the last word. No, a check for ice cream wasn't much of a last word, but under the circumstances it was the best she could do.

Damn it, this wasn't the way it should have worked out. Not only had Sylvie's little ploy upset his mother, it had disrupted an important medical operation. All things considered, Dr Bonaventura had been very good about it. Much better than he would have been. She was actually pretty sexy when riled, he thought. Not that he'd intended to rile her. But he sure couldn't help but see the obvious.

Sexy aside, though, he felt sick about what he had to do. Thinking about all those children who wouldn't have their surgeries because of him...because of Sylvie...literally made him sick to his stomach. Suppose Sean had been one of those children? Suppose he'd been on a waiting list for a medical procedure only to be turned away because some selfish idiot of a woman had pulled a stupid stunt for money? Or some idiot of a man had never seen it coming?

Damn, he cursed himself for this as much as he did Sylvie. And in the meantime, a whole lot of innocent people were going to suffer. That was inexcusable. Absolutely inexcusable!

Adrian paid the bill then stepped out onto the street and spotted Caprice and Isabella fairly flying down the sidewalk. They were trying to get away from him, and he couldn't blame them. What he'd just done wasn't a very noble thing. In fact, it was downright despicable and he was embarrassed. "Ben," he said, cellphone to his ear, as he followed them. "Suppose something detained me here and I couldn't get home right away?"

"What do you mean?" his attorney asked.

"Realistically, how much help can I be if I come back to Miami today? Is there anything I can do to help find Sylvie and get Sean back?"

"Not much. I've got my best investigator on it, and the truth is, unless Sylvie wants to be found, there's a good chance she won't be until she's damn good and ready. She wants to take you good this time, and you know what I've got to say about that."

"Same thing you always say. Take it to court. Try and get all her parental privileges revoked. But you know what I've got to say about that."

"I know. You want to protect Sean from all the ugliness, and I do understand that, Adrian. But until you can legally put Sylvie in her place, this is going to happen over and over. Also, if you think that having her take Sean with her is going to traumatize him any less than what he's going through, being torn in half by the two of you, you're sadly mistaken. Sylvie wants it all, and if she doesn't succeed this time, next time's only going to be worse. And Sean will be the one to suffer then, too. Bottom line is, you can't protect him any more. He's old enough to understand what this is about, and while you've fought a hard battle and done a good job taking care of him and protecting him, it's out of your control now. Sylvie's seen to that."

That much was true. Ben was right. "I'll give it some thought, and we'll talk about it when I'm back in the States. For now, I don't want the police involved, if there's any way we can get around it."

"They're not particularly interested, so I don't see any reason to drag them in. Like I said, I've got the best investigator on it money can buy. If Sylvie's anywhere to be found, Paul Radke will find her. And going back to your first question about how much you're needed here—my advice is to stay where you are. You're too hot-headed when it comes to Sylvie. I don't want you dealing with her yet. Especially if we're going to position ourselves to get her into court at some time in the future."

True again. He did tend to lose his temper where his ex-wife was concerned. Every time he did, she benefitted. From his bank account to her pocketbook.

"Communications aren't good where I'm going. At least not by cellphone."

"They have land lines and computers, don't they?"

Grudgingly, Adrian conceded that they did. He really did want to go home, to be there for Sean when Sylvie brought him back, to take Sylvie to task one more time. But there was Caprice Bonaventure and Operation Smiling Faces to consider, too, and she didn't deserve the fallout from this war between Sylvie and him. Neither did the children.

Steadying himself with a deep breath, Adrian doubled his pace to catch up to Caprice. "I'll give you all my contact numbers and references as soon as I get to the hospital," he told Ben.

"Good decision."

"Then why the hell am I not feeling good about it?" he grunted.

"I'll handle it, Adrian. Don't worry. You know Sean's safe with her. And if I need you here for any reason, I'll let you know."

That was the way they left it, and as Adrian tucked his cellphone back in his pocket, he wasn't sure what he felt. He was sick over leaving Sean behind. Caprice had Isabelle here, and if Sylvie hadn't interfered so much he'd have had Sean here, too. He was also worried. What father wouldn't be? His son was missing. Safe or not with Sylvie, Sean wasn't where he was supposed to be. That's the only thing that counted here. So maybe Ben was right. Maybe it *was* time to bring an end to Sylvie's involvement.

Or bring an end to his own if Sylvie had a mind to do it, as, after all, he really wasn't Sean's father.

"I thought he was nice," Isabella said, as Caprice slowed down a little once they were away from the ice-cream shop.

"Nice, maybe, but when you make a promise you're supposed to keep it." Like Tony had promised to be a father to Isabella, even after the divorce. Like Adrian had promised to be her anesthesiologist. Other things always got in the way, didn't they? And it was so easy to drop the really important matters when they did. Tony did without a flinch, and Adrian had without even the batting of an eyelash. So had her father, in so many ways.

Which was why she didn't get involved with men on any level. She just didn't trust them. Simple as that. Keep them at an arm's length personally, let them stand in their professional place with her, but nothing else. That kept Isabella safe. Kept *her* safe, too.

Fighting the urge to look back to see if Adrian was watching them, and she knew he was from the feel of the prickly goosebumps popping out on her arms, Caprice turned the corner and spotted the little landing strip at the private airport. Grant Makela was there, leaning casually against the airplane, eating a mango. Baggy khaki shorts hanging down to his knees, red and yellow Hawaiian print cotton shirt, sandals… Nice guy, Grant. He worked in a clinic on Oahu. Born and raised there, he was good for a couple weeks away from the islands before he got homesick and went back. But she could count on him for two trips during the year. Being a pilot helped, too. One of the local ranchers donated the plane, and Grant flew it when necessary.

He was truly one of the few men she did trust. Not her type, in his overly casual ways. But she liked him. Like a brother. And right now she couldn't get to the plane fast enough. All she wanted was to leave San José and put the whole, ugly scene with Adrian McCallan miles behind her. Of course, what she was about to face wasn't good—so many people to let down. But there was nothing she could do about that.

"Caprice!"

She heard the shout from behind her. Recognized the voice. Ignored it.

"Slow down. I want to talk to you."

She didn't want to talk to him, though. Not any more. What was there to talk about?

"Adrian wants us to stop, Mommy," Isabella said, trying to tug her mother to a stop. "Mommy! We *have* to stop!" she cried, when Caprice only quickened her pace.

"If he wants to talk to me, he'll have to catch up," she replied stiffly, upping her pace even more, even though Isabella was trying to slow her down.

"Why don't you l-like him?"

"I don't know him well enough to like or dislike him," she lied. Truth was, from that first tug of attraction until now, she simply didn't know what she felt about Adrian. If he did have problems at home, and she certainly did understand problems at home as she'd had her fair share, she was being much too harsh about this. And as for the way Isabella acted toward him…well, the child liked him, and she was old enough to have her own opinions. Although Isabella's quick reaction to Adrian did worry her some.

Still, what was it that had her nearly running away from a man she'd only just met?

"Look, Caprice, I don't blame you for being angry, but I've made arrangements to stay."

That stopped her. Dead in her tracks, actually. Taking a firmer grip on Isabella's hand, she turned around slowly to face him. "So now you want to stay?" she snapped. "Quit one minute, come back the next?"

"I always wanted to stay," he defended himself. "I didn't

think my circumstances would allow it, but I've made some arrangements that'll let me stay here."

She should have been glad to hear it, and deep down she was, but she still wasn't able to react the way she should. Something about the man put her on the defensive. "Arrangements you could have made before you let me know how little you think of your obligation to Operation Smiling Faces? You're *not* making a good first impression here, Doctor."

He cocked an eyebrow at her, and she couldn't tell if the look was speculative, angry or amused. And that put her on the defensive all the more. "We're a serious operation, and we deserve more respect than you're giving us. I'm not so sure I want someone working with us who has an obvious lack of real concern for what we do, as you seem to."

"You talk a lot, Doctor," he said, his face dead serious even though a twinkle was in his dark eyes. "And say all the wrong things for someone who, only a few minutes ago, wanted me to stay."

Standing there doing nothing more than staring at her, he was disarming her. Disarmed in one twinkle. Bad sign. Very bad sign, and she drew in a sharp breath to steady her resolve. "You expect me to grovel and slobber out a thank you after what you've put me through? Is that what this is about now? You're trying to humble me, trying to put me in my place?"

"This is me trying to extend a sincere apology and honor my commitment. And what I expect you to do is get me to Operation Smiling Faces the fastest way you can." He stepped up next to Isabella, who immediately latched onto his hand. "I'm sorry we got off to a bad start, and even more sorry about almost leaving. None of it is what I'd intended to happen, but it did, and all I can do is keep on apologizing. Or go to the hospital and start work, if you'll have me. Your choice, Caprice. Do I stay, or do I go?"

In answer, Caprice started off toward the airplane, she holding one of Isabella's hands, he holding the other. Neither Caprice nor

Adrian spoke, but sandwiched between them, Isabella was smiling for all she was worth.

The flight was smooth enough, and Grant was certainly a fine pilot, but basically Caprice hated flying and hated flying in these little planes even more. Good thing for the Dramamine already in her system. She never flew without it. Good thing for the earphones, too, and the drone of Mozart from the CD player in her ears. None of this actually alleviated all her nervousness over stepping into an oversized tin can and having somebody hurl it straight into the air, but anything, short of tranquilizers, which she never took, that calmed her down and got rid of the nausea was just fine with her.

Isabella had gone to sleep almost immediately after they'd left the landing strip. She was curled up in the seat across from Caprice, totally oblivious to all the things that were currently making Caprice jumpy. Just as well. Poor child had enough problems without heaping her own phobia on top of them.

And Adrian… When he wasn't sitting with a scowl on his face and a black cloud hanging over his head, he was shouting medical talk at Grant over the clatter of the engine. And so it went for the entire trip. When they finally landed on the grass strip cut into the thick of the jungle outside Golfito, Caprice was ready to get out and kiss the ground, she was so happy to be back.

"You don't like flying much, do you?" Adrian asked, taking the sleeping child from the seat and carrying her to the door.

Caprice stepped up to take Isabella away from him, but he didn't give her that choice. Instead, he exited the plane carrying her, taking obvious pains not to jostle or awaken her. Then when they were all on the ground and Caprice made another attempt to take Isabella, he shrugged her off.

"I can do that," she whispered.

He smiled. "So can I, and for me she's not so heavy."

Caprice wasn't sure what to make of it. Was he being considerate, or was he trying to impose himself into a place he didn't belong? Maybe her need to over-protect was causing her to read more into a simple gesture than was there. "I hate flying," she said, falling into step with Adrian as they crossed the grass on the way to the pickup truck sent to fetch them. "Always have. Always will."

"There are pills for that," he said.

"I could get liquored up, too, but I don't. It's easier to listen to Mozart. Better for the body, too."

Adrian gave Caprice a sideways glance, one that extended from head to toe—one she was not unaware of—then returned his focus to the truck ahead. "Look, I know we're off to a bad start here, and I'm sorry about that. Since I've decided to stay, I'd like for us to find some way to have a cordial working relationship."

"Since you've decided to stay?" she snapped. "Your first choice is to *not* be here. I don't know what changed your mind and kept you here, Dr McCallan, and truthfully I don't want to know. We don't get into other people's personal business. But as for that cordial working relationship you want…our working relationships here don't have outside factors coming into them. We don't allow that. We have a lot of work to do in a very short time, and distractions are costly. So if you want cordial, that's fine. But as for your bad start, that's not so easily forgotten. You nearly threw us into a position that would have damaged us, and it was clear that staying here and honoring your obligation wasn't important enough to you. And even now you're only here because something else came up that kept you from going home. That didn't get past me, Dr McCallan. So, as far as I'm concerned, you can be as sorry as you want, but I'm wary and I'm going to stay wary until you prove yourself to me. Now, would you, please, hand me my daughter?"

"Do you hate all men, or is it just me?" he asked, still hanging onto the sleeping girl.

Caprice narrowed her eyes in anger. "This mission is about the children, Dr McCallan. That's *all* it's about. You don't get to ask me personal questions."

"So do you like your work?" he asked, stopping next to the old, green, dented, rusty truck and turning to face Caprice.

"I said no questions."

A slight smile tugged at the corners of his mouth. "You said personal questions. Asking you about your work is totally professional."

Caprice opened the door to the passenger section behind the front seat and climbed in, then stretched out her arms to take Isabella. "How I feel about my work is highly personal, Dr McCallan," she said as he slid the child over to her. Then, instead of continuing the discussion between them, or the argument, depending upon the perspective, she slammed the door shut, leaving Adrian to climb into the front seat with Grant and a local named Don Pepe, who'd volunteered to bring the truck to the landing strip.

No one said a word all the way to the hospital, partly because Isabella was still sleeping soundly—sleeping the way only a child could under the circumstances—and partly because Caprice's bad mood seem to permeate even the rusty metal of the old truck. It wasn't rational, the way she was feeling. She knew that. She even tried to force herself into a better mood, but something about Adrian McCallan was setting her off, and she simply didn't know what it was. Meaning there was no way to put it right. She tried convincing herself that his preference to leave was the reason but, honestly, she knew better. That was only part of it, and the rest was a great big blank.

Sleep. After a good night of it things would be better tomorrow. She was sure of that. Well, not so sure as much as she *hoped* that would be the case. Because one thing was certain. If she didn't get over it, working with Adrian McCallan was going to be impossible.

Briefly, she wondered if him going back to Miami might have been better for all concerned.

"I don't know what you did to her," Grant Makela said, showing Adrian to his little room. It was a sparse cell—bed, bathroom, chair, closet. Nothing inviting. Nothing nice. Just basic living space in the hospital resident quarters. "One of the reasons we all come out is because of Caprice. She's extraordinary. Such passion." He tossed Adrian's duffle in the door. "She was pretty cheerful when we went to San José, but now…" He shrugged. "All I can say is good luck. She's scheduled you to be on her surgical team, meaning the two of you are going to working in some pretty tight quarters. With the way she's acting right now, all I can say is better you than me."

"That ought to be fun, the two of us in the OR," Adrian replied, thinking about the corrosive way in which the two of them had started. It was his fault entirely. He admitted that. Regretted it. But Caprice was as stubborn a woman as he'd ever met, and she wasn't going to give him any mercy. Briefly, he wondered if anybody had ever earned her forgiveness.

Grant shrugged. "Well, whatever it is, I hope you get it worked out pretty soon, as we've got a full docket to get us started. Starting at seven tomorrow morning, by the way. And brace yourself for some long days. We work, on average, sixteen hours. Sometimes more. People are already lining up outside."

Adrian went to the window and pulled back the blinds. Sure enough, there was a single line with about thirty people standing in it—mothers and fathers with children, grandparents, brothers and sisters—all people affected by a facial deformity in their lives. All there with the same purpose. "They'll be here all night?" he asked.

"Some of them have been here since this morning. They come prepared for this."

"But you won't be able to see them all."

"One way or another, everybody gets seen. Whether or not all the children get scheduled for a procedure is another thing. We prioritise. First, severity. Is the deformity affecting a substantial life issue like eating or drinking? Second, age. Caprice is very sensitive to how cruel people can be to children with facial deformities and she also knows that the older the child gets the more hurtful people can become, so she likes to get to the older children as soon as she can. Then another priority is the children who are likely to be abandoned because of the way they look, or may have already been abandoned. They go to the top of the list, too."

"Then it's not just about the procedure."

Grant laughed. "Once you've been around for a couple of days, you'll learn that there's much more to this than only the medical procedure." He glanced at his watch. "Look, it's going to start early, and I'm ready to turn in for the night. If you're hungry, there's a staff lounge down the hall. Refrigerator is full. We keep it stocked as there won't be any regularly scheduled meals, so help yourself. And I'll see you bright and early." With that, he gave Adrian a salute, backed out the door and closed it after him, leaving Adrian standing in the middle of his sparse room, wondering just what in the world he'd volunteered to do.

He didn't stand there thinking for too long, however. Once he'd shoved his foldable clothes into a drawer and hung up the rest in the closet, he left his room and hurried down the hall in search of a telephone. His first few hours with Caprice Bonaventura had gotten off to a rocky start, but maybe there would be some good news from home. Maybe Sylvie had come to her senses, brought Sean back, and life was back to normal.

She was always restless the night before they opened the clinic. Tonight she was even more restless than usual. Probably because she was tired. Probably because she wasn't sure that, come morning, her anesthesiologist would still be there. Certainly, he'd started off on the wrong foot, and not just by almost leaving. Actually, it wasn't that he was mean or grumpy or had any personality traits that truly rubbed her the wrong way either. It's just that, well…she didn't know what it was. More than that, she didn't want to think about it.

Taking a look to make sure Isabella was fast asleep, Caprice decided to wander down to the cafeteria and scrounge a cup of coffee. There was always a pot brewing, and while a good jolt of caffeine wasn't what she needed to calm her nerves, just sitting and relaxing might help. So she let Josefina, Isabella's caregiver, know where she was going before she trotted off to the cafeteria. Josefina—she counted her blessings for that woman! She was a smart, sharp-tongued, outspoken, grandmotherly woman who truly loved Isabella. Caprice had known her since the first time she'd come to Costa Rica, nearly five years ago, and counted her as a dear friend. In fact, Caprice trusted her with Isabella as much as she trusted her own mother. If not for Josefina's devotion, these long trips wouldn't have been possible as Caprice would not have left her daughter home in California for more than a week or two. Not even with her own mother. Yes, the woman was truly a godsend, she thought as she closed the door behind her and scurried down the hall.

The cafeteria was dim inside when she got there, with only the minimum of lighting turned on. And so quiet that the faint electrical hum of the vending machines and refrigerator seemed almost an intrusion. A very nice mood here for the middle-of-the-night coffee craving, she thought as she found the coffee-pot, poured herself a cup, and took a seat at the table in the corner. It was obscured from almost everything else in the room by the vending machines, and she was glad to tuck herself away to be alone for this little while. She rarely got to do that, rarely got to have time to herself.

Sighing, she took her first sip of coffee, then settled back into the hard-backed metal chair and stared up at the green light from the coin return on the candy-bar machine reflecting off the ceiling. On the other side of the room, voices entering whispered in muffled tones, apparently in respect for the quiet atmosphere there.

Ten minutes. That's all she would allow herself, then she'd return to Isabella, and try to get some sleep, too. Or else she'd be all baggy-eyed and sluggish come morning.

"You really do like doing this, don't you?" he asked, his voice coming out of nowhere.

Caprice startled. "I didn't see you," she gasped, immediately bolting upright.

"I saw you," Adrian said, taking a seat next to her. Without invitation. "You're wound up pretty tightly for a woman who has a large medical operation ready to start in the morning."

"I'm always like this the night before. There's so much to do, and I'm afraid I'll overlook something, or miss someone who needs to be seen. A lot of people depend on our trips down here, and…" Why was she telling him all this? It seemed that she was always babbling on around him. He had that kind of effect on her. Wary, yet babbling away. Odd mix.

"Somehow I don't see you overlooking anything. My guess is that you're obsessive over detail."

"Not obsessive. Just careful." Maybe a little obsessive, but she wasn't going to babble on about that, too.

He chuckled. "There's a fine line, and you're over it, Dr Bonaventura. You couldn't do otherwise."

"What makes you think you know me so well?" she snapped, that strange response to him clicking on with a slight chill wiggling up her spine.

"Takes one look. Over-protective mother, a doctor passionate to her cause. How could you not be obsessive?"

"Protective," she corrected. "Not over-protective."

He chuckled again, then took a sip of his own coffee. "Your eyes practically popped out of their sockets when Isabella took to me. Oh, you were polite about it. But you were bothered. Admit it."

"You're a stranger. I've taught her never to talk to strangers."

"It's hard for children to make the distinction between strangers and friends when the person they trust most in the world introduces that stranger into their life. Child trusts parent, therefore child trusts parent's judgment. You brought me into Isabella's life and she trusted that."

He surprised her, sounding so insightful in matters to do with children. Of course, his own medical practice was devoted to children, so that was probably the reason. He worked with them every day. "Are you to be trusted, Dr McCallan?"

"Depends, I suppose."

"On what?"

"To what aspects of my life are you referring? Medically, as a doctor, I'm absolutely to be trusted. Personally, as a friend, I've never had anyone say I'm not trustworthy."

"But as a man?" she asked, immediately regretting it. That had just slipped out. Some of her true sentiments shining through, the ones she never, ever let loose around any aspect of her professional life.

"I'd say that's pretty revealing," he answered. "A mother alone in the Costa Rican jungle with her daughter. No wedding ring on her finger. Very distrustful of men. I'd say those are all signs of a relationship ending very badly."

"And I'd say those are personal things I don't discuss."

"But didn't you open the door to that conversation by asking me if I'm trustworthy as a man? That seems like personal conversation to me, and if you're allowed to indulge in it, in all fairness, I should be given the same consideration." He sat his cup down on the table and stretched his long legs out in front of him. "And the answer to your question is yes. As a man, I can be trusted. So now it's your turn. You owe me one. Did the relationship end badly?"

She glared across at him, and even though the room was dim, she could see the intense look on his face. He was serious. He really did expect an answer. "Why do you want to know?" she asked.

"Because I like to know with whom I'm dealing. My reading on you before I came here didn't reveal much. Mostly academic credits, medical accomplishments. Certainly nothing about Caprice the person. By design, I'm sure."

"And why would knowing more about Caprice *the person* benefit you?"

"I'm not answering any more of your questions until you answer mine. In this world, you always have to give a little something to get something."

Caprice huffed out an impatient sigh. Her time was up. She needed to get back to Isabella. "In this world, sometimes it's nice to give something without expecting anything in return for it." With that, she stood, then looked down at him. "And in answer to your question, yes. It ended badly. As badly as a marriage could possibly end." Then she left him sitting there.

When she got out into the hall she slumped against the wall, thinking about putting her burning cheeks up against the cool cement blocks to stop the heat. Instead, though, she took a deep breath, squared her shoulders, and fairly ran to her room before anyone had a chance to see how badly she was blushing. And shaking. And going wobbly in the knees.

From the end of that same hallway Adrian stood in the cafeteria doorway, watching Caprice make her hasty retreat. When she finally disappeared through her door, he returned to the public telephone to make yet another try at a call home.

CHAPTER THREE

THE room was basic. One great, open area partitioned into separate exam spaces by curtains, with each cordoned space containing a stainless-steel exam table, a stool for the doctor and a chair for the child's parent, blood-pressure cuff, hand disinfectant, gloves—the most basic of medical equipment. Minimally equipped, yet equipped well enough.

Near the main entrance to the room stood several rows of brown folding chairs, all set up in neat long rows for parents and children awaiting their turn with one of the doctors. And there was a play area in the corner with donated bright red, blue and green plastic toys for the youngest children. It was always the most popular spot in the room—a place for them to come together to make new friends.

When the room wasn't in use as a mass exam for Operation Smiling Faces, it served as a hall for hospital meetings and in-service training sessions—a multi-purpose room in function with three white cement block walls and a fourth wall that was more a row of windows overlooking the lush Costa Rican jungle.

Caprice liked the room. Over the many times she'd been here, she'd come to appreciate the sparse quality of it, and even taken it on as a symbol of their mission—basic, without extras, minimally equipped, yet equipped well enough to give the children what they needed. No one complained that, in surgical sequences which would require multiple procedures, the entirety of the medical treatment might be spread out months, even years longer than it would elsewhere. The people here weren't like that. They weren't impatient or presumptuous. Rather, they were kind, friendly and, most of all, appreciative.

Perhaps that's why she kept coming back. In truth, she loved the smiles. One smile on a face that had never before smiled made all the effort worth everything it took to reach the medical end.

The medical end…even her own Isabella hadn't reached the end yet. She would require more surgeries over time as her face matured. The same with many of these children. Tweaks to compensate for growth, maybe another scar reduction depending on how technology advanced. More dental work. But then, somewhere, came a logical, beautiful end to it—an end everyone in this room wanted badly. Including herself, for them, and for Isabella.

This morning, Caprice had ordered all the blinds closed as there were so many people now waiting outside those windows. Many more than last night. Hopefuls who didn't have a scheduled appointment but came anyway, in the expectation that their child might find a place on the ever-growing appointment list. Sighing as she shut the last of the blinds on the more than one hundred people out there, Caprice turned back to face her team. "It gets bigger and bigger every time we're here," she said, smiling. It didn't bother her. In fact, it rather pleased her that she was trusted here.

"All facial disfigurations?" Adrian asked.

"No. About half the people here know there's some kind of free medical treatment being given to children, so they bring their children no matter what's wrong. Tonsillitis, common virus, skin rashes. Sometimes nothing's wrong at all."

"Sometimes the adults try to pass themselves off as children," Grant Makela commented, laughing.

"And?" Adrian asked.

"If it's simple," Grant replied, "and we have time, we take care of them. If it's anything more than a scratch or a bump, anything requiring real treatment, we refer them to the hospital."

Caprice nodded her agreement. "Medical standards are good here in Costa Rica, but there are always poor people in need no matter where you go, and in this area the medical facilities aren't adequate for the overall need," Caprice said, then smiled. "You can't blame people for trying. I'd probably do the same." In her heart she knew there would have been nothing she wouldn't have done to find help for Isabella. More than anyone else in this group could realize, Caprice did understand that need in a parent.

"And if the hospital won't see them?" Adrian asked.

"Then there's nothing we can do."

"In other words, we let them walk away!"

He sounded exasperated—much more so than he should have. Truth was, he'd known the protocol before he'd come. So why was he on the verge of arguing with her? Caprice's brow knit with curiosity rather than anger over his near-challenge. "That's not fair, Doctor. Each and every one of us gives everything we have to this cause, but that doesn't always work out for the people who want to see us. I wish it did, but it doesn't." My, but he was irritable this morning. Irritable and, from the looks of that scowl clamping down over his face, itching to pick a fight with someone. Well, not her, not now. She didn't have time. "We do the best we can do and hope it's enough."

"And the best we can do is send them out the door with a pat on the back and good wishes?" he continued.

Caprice finally leveled a cool stare at Adrian. Well, so much for forcing the situation between them. "You send them to me and I'll make the decisions. At this stage of the operation your *only* job is to do a preliminary exam and give me your opinion. Do you understand me, Dr McCallan? The one, and only, thing I want from you is your medical opinion. I'll take care of the decisions."

Instead of reacting with a comeback or even a frown, he merely stared back at her, nearly as cooly as she stared at him. And didn't speak.

One problem doctor out of the bunch. She'd had them before—the ones who knew better than everybody else. The ones whose opinions were the only ones that mattered—or so they thought. In the scheme of things it was easier to leave those types alone and let them do their work. Most were here only two weeks, and for what she got out of them in those two weeks, Caprice found it much easier to allow them their attitudes and opinions and bad moods. In the end she was still in charge, and she still made the final decisions regarding each and every patient they took on. She knew that, and normally she took care not to flaunt it. Yet something about Adrian made her want to flaunt it. Or need to.

She watched him standing by the window, brooding, and desperately hoped that he wasn't going to present any problem worse than his attitude and mood. Those she could handle, but anything else…

"So, as some of you know, and others may have already observed, there are ten doctors out on this trip. Four surgeons, four anesthesiologists, and two general practitioners. Also along are a group of ten nurses, surgical techs and general medics. Next week I'll have three dental surgeons coming in." This was her largest group ever and, judging from the numbers of people lining up outside, she worried if it would be enough. "So, we all know what to do for starters. Find your exam space, and one of the volunteers will start showing patients in. Do a preliminary physical exam, all the standard things, note any other physical observations you find, and based upon what you see, make a recommendation." She glanced at Adrian, who'd completely turned his back to her now, and was focused on the line of people waiting outside. "We'll each do general duty today and tomorrow, and go to a third day if necessary. Children who meet the criteria for surgery will be sent to me and children who need medical care not connected to Operation Smiling Faces will be sent to Dr Makela for further evaluation. Any questions?"

She looked straight at Adrian, expecting something from him, but his back was still to her. "Well, then. Good luck. If you need anything, or have any questions, I'll be in the private exam room across the hall." That was where she made the final determinations, where she accepted children for facial reconstruction or rejected them. Broke the good news, or the bad, to the hopeful parents and eager children. Gave that pat on the back and good wishes, as Adrian had called it. "Dr McCallan, could I see you in my office in five minutes?" she asked, then signaled for Isabella, who was anxious to go off to the play area with Josefina.

"So, is this where you dole out the punishment for me being out of line?" Adrian asked, strolling into Caprice's office and shutting the door behind him.

It was a small office, stark. One desk, two chairs. An exam table. No window. Adrian gave it a quick scan then plunked himself down on the edge of the stainless-steel exam table.

"No. This is where I give you the opportunity to tell me what the bad attitude is about." Like he would! But she figured that was as good an opening as any.

"You consider being inquisitive a bad attitude?"

She'd hoped he might have mellowed out, but apparently he hadn't. "I consider the way you challenged me in front of the others a bad attitude. Or bad manners."

"I simply asked about turning people away."

"You simply implied that turning people away goes against the Hippocratic oath."

"And doesn't it?" His voice was sharp-edged, but not hostile.

"If that's the kind of medicine you wish to practice, Doctor, I admire that. It would be wonderful to think we could take on every medical problem that falls into our laps while we're here. But we're not equipped to do that. We don't have the funding, and more than that we don't have the medical sanction to do so. We're here for a specific reason. Our organization establishes that and the Costa Rican government welcomes it. And that's what we do. We have a certain amount of latitude in some areas, but our goal is not to run roughshod over the local medical establishment and authorities. So, after your service here has ended, you're free to take your medical bag and set up whatever kind of practice you want. Do it here in Costa Rica if you'd like. But while you're serving as a representative of Operation Smiling Faces you'll work by the dictates of the organization."

"I didn't intend to step on toes," he said, the sharpness flowing away from his voice. "Sorry if I did. I was overwhelmed by the sheer number of people lining up outside."

An apology? He'd actually given her an apology of sorts? She'd expected a fight, a real banger from him. But this wasn't the man she'd gone up against a few minutes ago. He'd changed back to the man she'd thought he was. "Apology accepted, and I understand how you feel. I'm constantly overwhelmed. Makes me grumpy sometimes, too, that I can't do more." Caprice was totally thrown off by this turnaround in him as she still had another good speech to throw at him. "Look, Adrian, I know we're not getting off to an exactly brilliant start between us, but is something wrong? Something I can help with? You seem worried, and if there's anything I can do…"

He stood up from the table and headed toward the door. "Like I said, I was out of line and I'm sorry about that. It won't happen again, and if it does, you're welcome to call me out on it. I'll deserve it. There's no excuse for rude behavior and you shouldn't tolerate it from me." His voice was strange. On the verge of turning emotional, yet with so much held back. As he walked away from her, Caprice was left with the unsettling feeling that there were many things Adrian McCallan was holding back. Of course, by her own rules, that was none of her business.

"Look, I'm about to get busy. I'll be tied up for hours and I don't know when I'll be able to call you again. So, what have you learned?" He wasn't expecting anything. It was too early yet for Sylvie to give up. Not when she wanted everything he had this time. Sylvie was cunning. She was also smart, and she knew exactly what she was doing, taking Sean away at this time. She'd counted on Adrian not going back on his word to Operation Smiling Faces. Conscience always got the better of him and she'd figured that out years ago. Or else why would they have stayed married as long as they had? He'd been the one insisting on making a go of it, trying to be the perfect family for Sean. He'd been the one making the sacrifices to do the right thing, and Sylvie had latched onto that like a mosquito latches onto sweaty flesh and sucks the blood right out.

It had been his blood being drained throughout their marriage.

And now Sylvie also knew he wouldn't come after her directly, but would be forced to have someone else do it for him, and that he wouldn't take this to the police or have a warrant sworn out for her. There were too many threats in place, making his need to protect Sean an easy way for Sylvie to manipulate what she wanted. What she always got. She used it every chance she got.

This time she was counting on getting everything he had, which was why she was drawing her game out so long. She wanted Adrian to worry. She wanted him to become frantic…so frantic he would be anxious to turn over every last cent in his bank account. She wanted him begging to turn over every last cent just to get Sean back.

"Nothing to report, Adrian," his attorney told him. "Sorry, but so far we haven't come up with a trace of her."

"When she's ready," Adrian muttered.

"When she's ready, we'll be ready, too," Ben Rafferty said.

"I haven't changed my mind about not wanting the police in on this," Adrian warned. "I can't have Sean dragged into the middle of something like that." The biggest thing Sean had to be protected from now was *knowing* the kind of woman his mother was. That was a task getting more difficult every day. And with this latest antic of hers…

Adrian and his attorney talked for the next couple of minutes, until Adrian's first patient peeked around the curtain partition. That's when it began. Her name—Mayela. Mayela with big, beautiful dark eyes. Exquisite eyes with so much hope in them. Beautiful black hair, long, nearly to her waist, and straight. She was clasping a teddy bear to her chest and trying to smile through an obviously cleft lip. Through a volunteer interpreter, he asked Mayela's mother, "Does she speak English?" The woman was almost as shy as her daughter.

"She doesn't speak," Mayela's mother replied quietly, her words interpreted with the same inflection and emotion.

Adrian's heart lurched. Mayela was probably close to Sean's age. Suddenly he was filled with sadness over missing Sean as well as sadness for this lovely child here who had never yet spoken. "But I'll bet once we fix things up for you, you'll be talking like everyone else, won't you, Mayela?"

She nodded her head, still clasping her teddy as tightly as she could.

"So right now the first thing we've got to do is take a look at you to make sure you're strong and healthy." He pointed Mayela's mother to a chair next to the wall, then explained, "This will only take a few minutes, and I promise it won't hurt."

Mayela seemed to accept that because she willingly

climbed up on the exam table and allowed Adrian to listen to her chest with the stethoscope. Once he'd determined that her heart was sound, he let Mayela have a listen, then explained to her what that noise was. She was fascinated, captivated, and before she was done, she was listening to Adrian's heart, then her mother's, then the interpreter's—a girl named Ana, who wasn't much more than a child herself. Afterwards, she handed the stethoscope back to Adrian, and pointed to the blood-pressure cuff.

Rather than spending another five minutes allowing the child to play with it, and getting caught up in that play himself, he handed it to her without explanation and set about his work while she tried to figure it out. Throughout the physical exam he asked the girl's mother questions about Mayela's general health then, after he was satisfied that she was a normal, healthy child in almost every aspect, he dashed off a few preliminary notes. Instead of handing them to the volunteer runner who was supposed to carry them across the hall to Caprice's office, Adrian took them himself, leaving Mayela behind, still curious about the blood-pressure cuff. A budding doctor, he decided as he opened Caprice's door.

"You didn't have to bring these records yourself," Caprice said, gesturing for him to set the notes on her desk.

"I want her to have surgery," he said. "She's deserving. Healthy, bright, eager. Supportive mother."

"They're all deserving," Caprice said, barely looking up at him.

"They're waiting for your decision."

"All of them are, Adrian. And I'm pretty quick about it. I've got three other cases to review ahead of yours, then I'll—"

"She's seven years old, and she's never talked," he interrupted.

This caught Caprice's attention. "But you said she's healthy in every other aspect?"

He nodded. "I promised her surgery."

"You're not supposed to promise her anything."

"Then tell me how to do that after working with the child, Caprice, because I sure as hell don't know."

Caprice gave him a questioning look, cocking her head to the side to stare up at him. She stared for a full thirty seconds, no expression whatsoever visible on her face, until finally she spoke. "Welcome to Operation Smiling Faces, Adrian. I wasn't sure you were going to make it. You've got an attitude I don't understand, I'm not at all sure about your commitment level, but you've made it." She stood and extended her hand to him. "I'm Caprice Bonaventura, one of the surgeons in the group. I've stood where you stood, seen what you saw."

"And what's that supposed to mean?" he snapped, letting her hand dangle in mid-air.

"It's supposed to mean that you've got the passion, which is good. If you hadn't barged in to plead your first case, I would have pulled you off exam duty and put you in the equipment room to take inventory or some other out-of-the-way job."

He raised his eyebrows skeptically. "So I passed your test?"

"In the ways that count, yes. You passed." Her smile turned warm. "And I'm glad you did," she said, her voice low and as friendly as he'd heard it. "Although I'm not sure why," she added almost under her breath.

She was glad? That was out of character for her. Nice, but out of character. But he was glad, too. "Good to meet you, Caprice," Adrian said, finally accepting her hand. Soft, gentle. Her grasp was almost a caress as she slipped her hand into his then back out again. It caught him off guard—not the feel of her hand so much as his reaction to it. "Um…it…it looks like I'll be sitting at the head of your surgical table," he began, trying not to stumble too hard over his words, "unless the boss here has me counting bedpans and tongue depressors and doing other out-of-the-way jobs. She's a mean one, I hear." And so gorgeous she nearly blinded him. Gorgeous aside, he wasn't sure what to make of the way she kept her personal side off limits because what had just happened there, that little interchange between them, seemed very on limits. Subtle, but real. "But she has possibilities, I'm told." *If you knew how to find her good side.*

"And who told you that?"

Had that been a playful arch of the eyebrows she'd just tossed at him? Or merely a speculative one? With Caprice, he couldn't tell. Which was probably for the best as he really didn't want the involvement that was popping into his mind right now. "Her daughter. Cute kid. Smart. Some very nice personal traits her mother could use herself."

"Except her mother doesn't do personal." The look he thought might have been a flirty one suddenly left Caprice's eyes and she sat back down. "So back to your patient. I'm glad you want to be her staunch advocate as that's what every one of these kids will need from us." She pulled Mayela's papers over and took a look. "Send her in," she finally said. "And don't make promises again, Adrian. We can't do that here, as much as we want to. Promises might have good intentions behind them, but they can also break hearts."

Was that a professional sentiment, he wondered, or a personal one? "Did you ever make a promise?" he asked on his way back to the hall.

"Once, a very long time ago."

"Did you keep it?"

She glanced at the picture of Isabella sitting on her desk, and a dewy look clouded her eyes. "I'm trying."

What was it about Adrian that played so hard on her emotions? One moment she almost hated the guy and the next she…well, she didn't know, but it wasn't hate. She'd positively flirted with the man one moment then nearly gone teary in front of him the next, for heaven's sake. One touch of his hand and here she was, all mushy. Then a little mention of a promise she'd made to herself so long ago—to Isabella, but first to her own sister—and she'd come close to letting it all go. It wasn't like her. Not at all. Even now, as she thought about it, the emotions were swirling— emotions that were either anger at herself, embarrassment, or simply worry that when Adrian was around she wasn't in the fullest control she demanded from herself.

Fullest control? Who was she kidding? There wasn't even a vestige of control in her when she was near him, and the worst part was, it didn't seem to matter. He walked in, had his way with her if only in a practical sense, and she was positively happy to let him do it. "I don't know what's going on with me," she said to her framed photo of Isabella—the one she carried with her everywhere she went. "But I don't like it."

Isabella had been smiling and happy that day three years ago. All had been right with her world. Her surgeries had been going beautifully, she had been delighted to make new little friends in the medical clinic—children suffering problems similar to Isabella's didn't ridicule others, didn't try to be cruel the way other children sometimes did. Of course, poor Isabella hadn't known that her father would turn out to be the cruelest of all people toward her, that he'd made plans to ship her off to boarding school so *he* wouldn't have to look at her face. His exact words had been, "She distracts my business partners when they come to our home. And you always insist that she be here, Caprice. But now I'm insisting that she's not."

His business partners…a group of fat, greedy real-estate in-vestors who smoked cigars and made rude remarks about women in general. Oh, she'd seen the looks they'd given Isabella. Seen the cringes, seen the turned-up noses in plain view of a child who didn't deserve that cruelty. Heard the unkind remarks they hadn't even tried to conceal…remarks laughed at by her husband. She had tried to keep Isabella away from all that, but the truth was, sometimes she hadn't been able to—*her* work, *his* scheduled appointments he hadn't told her about—and the inevitable had always happened then. Isabella had been hurt.

"I want her in a boarding school," Tony had said. "We can afford it, and we won't have to deal with her problems directly any more. We'll be better off for it. You'll see."

What she'd seen was divorce, however. But not right away. For a while Caprice had tried to block those hideous words from replaying in her head. Unfortunately, nothing had worked. Once they'd found their way back, and they always had, they couldn't be stopped. And with every last one of them she hated her ex-husband all the more.

"Mayela," Caprice said as Adrian's patient wandered into the office, clutching onto her mother with one hand and holding her teddy with the other. She glanced at Adrian's notes again, then at her own stamp of approval going to the file. "Let me explain what will be happening from here."

Adrian had good instincts, she decided as she watched the child hide herself behind her mother. Caprice could concede that much. Adrian had been right to insist on getting Mayela into surgery. So she gave him his due, but nothing else. *She hoped.*

"Long day," Caprice commented, taking a seat next to Adrian in the hospital dining room. Sixteen hours from the start of it, every one of them physically and emotionally exhausting. She slipped out of her shoes and pulled her feet up under her on the bench.

Adrian automatically glanced at his watch, even though he didn't have to. His body was screaming that he'd been at this far too long. "Longer than I've had in a while. Used to be able to do it better when I was a resident and they expected that many hours out of us routinely. Got into the habit of doing it. " He chuckled. "Of course, I was younger, too. Younger and in better shape." To him, it wasn't just a long day of work and so many children to see—each and every one of them reminding him of Sean in some little way. It had been a long day of missing Sean, and worrying about him. It had also been a long day of wanting to call Ben every ten minutes, but not being able to. Then, more than anything, it had been a long day of wondering how many wrong things he'd done as a father and trying to figure out if he'd done anything right. Right now, with such a big hole in his heart, he wasn't sure. "Good thing we do all that while we're still young enough, because there would be a shortage of doctors if we had to go through all that now."

He just wanted to go home, to join in the hunt. But he knew he couldn't, shouldn't, and still it didn't ease the pain of frustration over not being there. This had gone on long enough. It was time to find Sylvie and to get Sean away from her.

It was time to face the legal battles he'd been avoiding for so long, and know, one way or the other, what his standing with Sean would be. He was his father in all aspects except one. That was the single biggest worry he had in all this. Sean was his son, yet not biologically.

"They were tough years, but good ones, I thought," Caprice said, dipping her teabag into the hot water. "I liked my residency because that's when I had the first clear vision of what I wanted in my life. It's when I realized how I needed to go about it. Until that point I had done the course, done what had been expected, hoping that something good would follow."

"Medical school was expected from you? Not your choice?"

She frowned. "Oh, it was my choice. A promise I made to myself and my sis—*to myself* when I was young. My family thought I'd settle down into a nice, cozy pediatric practice or something like that. Surgery came as a shocker to the people who cared for me, and the type of surgery I chose…" Caprice smiled. "It was a good choice for me. I love what I do, but some of the people close to me were put off by it. So, what about you?" she asked, trying to get off the subject of herself. "Was medical school expected from you?"

Adrian laughed. "Both my parents were doctors, so the subject did come up every now and then. But there were also the days when I thought being an Olympic athlete might be nice, too. I always pictured myself with one of those medals around my neck, rather than a stethoscope."

"Really? What sport?"

"That was the problem. I wasn't particularly outstanding at any sport. Good enough at a lot of them, captain of the football team, modestly accomplished at tennis, not bad at several other things, but not good enough at any one of them to go on past school in them." He laughed. "I think my athletics was more about youthful rebellion than true desire, as I never thought they were worth working hard for. Also, I'm pretty sure my parents were glad that my true ambitions didn't lean in that direction. Although they never said anything."

"What was worth working hard for?"

"Until medical school, nothing. I found my niche there, much to my parents' happiness."

"Then it was a good thing you went to medical school."

"Most of the time I would agree with that." He stretched his arms out and moved them in circles, then flexed his back muscles and tilted his neck from side to side. "Until nights like this," he said on a weary yawn. "Then I wonder if I should have worked harder on lobbing those balls across the tennis net."

"Regrets?" she asked, flexing her own neck muscles as she fought back her own yawn.

"Not at all. I'm happy where I am. It's worked out, maybe not so much in the way of a youthful dream when you have these inflated images floating around in a wholly unused brain of what life should be, but in a very real way. And it's been good. So, what about you?"

She hesitated for a moment, her eyes drifting off to some-place far away. Then suddenly she snapped back to the present. "No regrets in any ways that matter. I love what I do. It makes a difference. It provides a good life for the two of us, and keeps us together in ways that many mothers and daughters will never be together. It's probably not the most normal of lives to most people, but for us it's just the way we live, and I don't have any regrets about any of it." She paused, smiled, then continued, "Of course, I probably should have divorced my no-good husband long before I did, and maybe I do have a little regret over hang-ing onto the bum for so long. Especially after I realized how well Isabella and I would do on our own. But hindsight and all that."

No man in the picture whatsoever? He thought about asking, and decided not to. This was further than he'd expected Caprice would go, talking about herself. A rather nice opener to a friend-ship, he thought. Or at least what he believed could be a friend-ship if she allowed it. "You don't happen to have an Internet hook-up I could use, do you?" he asked, deliberately changing the subject. "I brought my laptop along, but it won't work with the phone in my room, and I'm not really into the wireless age yet."

"In my office." She reached into her pocket and pulled out a key. "Lock up when you're done." With that, Caprice stood up, picked up her cup of coffee and left the dining room.

Damn good-looking woman, Adrian thought as he carried his cup of coffee out the door and headed to her office. Too bad he didn't let damn good-looking women into his life. But he'd done that once several years ago, and had paid the price every day since. A casual night here and there was one thing, but there wasn't a casual night in Caprice Bonaventura, and that's some-thing he'd just have to remember.

Caprice stared out the window at the dark outline of the jungle for a while, trying not to think about tomorrow and all the children she would see. Sometimes she just had to take a mental break from everything. It was hard to do when you were surrounded by your work, like she was, but it made her better at what she did. Gave her a fresh perspective when she tackled the next problem and the one after that.

Isabella was sound asleep now, and Josefina was curled up in a chair next to her bed, sound asleep, too. She didn't have the heart to awaken either one, so she shut the door to the little bedroom they were in and paced around the sitting room for an hour, wondering where this restlessness was coming from. Normally by now she was ready for a good sleep. But not tonight. She needed a walk. Or a nice hard run. Something was pent up inside her and she had a powerful need to work it out physically.

The exercise room. The hospital here did provide one for its doctors. A small one. One treadmill, a few weights, and some kind of pulley thing for the upper arms. Maybe that would hit the spot. She could run herself silly on the treadmill then come back and collapse into bed and have a good sleep in the remaining hours until she had to get up and start the routine all over again.

Without another thought she slipped out of her daily work cloths—cotton slacks, cotton shirt—and into a tracksuit. Then she refastened her hair into a knot at the back of her neck, slid into some running shoes, and went in pursuit of some physical torture, as she really wasn't one to take to the gym very often.

On her way down the hall she noticed that her office light was shining out from under the door. Had Adrian forgotten to turn it off? Instinctively, she pushed open her door, but what she found wasn't an empty office. Adrian was sitting at her desk, his back to the door, his laptop open and plugged into her phone line. Was he sleeping?

She studied his posture for a moment. Too rigid to be asleep. His breathing too normal. So what was it he could be concentrating on that distracted him so badly he hadn't even heard her come in?

For a moment Caprice thought about creeping back out and leaving him to whatever it was he was doing, but as she took a step backwards he spun around to face her. And the look on his face…indescribable in the blue glow of the LCD light from the computer monitor. "I didn't mean to disturb you," she said, her voice a whisper. This was an intrusion of some sort, and she did feel terribly awkward.

"Your office. You're allowed to disturb me."

His voice was odd. Too thick. Too somber. Nothing warm at all, like it usually was. "I thought you'd be in bed," she commented, backing her way out the door. It seemed like it should be one of those turn-around-and-run moments but yet, in some strange way, she was being pulled to him. Just the opposite of what she wanted.

"I thought *you'd* be in bed," he answered, his voice turning brittle.

"I was off to have a little jog on the treadmill," she explained, wondering why she felt the need to do so. "I couldn't sleep. Thought the exercise might do me some good." She owed this man nothing, yet something about him seemed to demand an explanation from her, something about him made her the intruder in her own office. It was like she'd come across an Adrian he hadn't meant anyone to see, and it was right that she apologize for it. The man was anguished, however. Even in the shadows she could see the look on his face…heartbreaking.

Caprice did understand the emotion all too well, although she didn't understand where it was coming from in Adrian, and every sinew in her body wanted to do something for him. But every bit of good sense told her to back all the way out into the hall, shut the door, go away. Leave him sitting alone in the dark, the way she'd found him. That's what he wanted as that's what she'd always wanted when she'd had her down moods, especially at the time she'd been divorcing Tony. The unspoken words to get out and leave him alone were heavy in the air. "I thought you'd left the light on," she said, trying to sound chipper. "But I see that you're still working, so I'll leave you alone and get on with what I was doing."

She almost expected him to say something. He almost looked like he wanted to. But he didn't, and she didn't wait around to see if he would. Instead, she pulled the door shut after her, and called back before it clicked shut, "See you in the morning, Doctor."

She heard his like response on top of the click. Immediately after, she stood in the hall, staring, for a moment, at the closed door, trying to shut out all the possibilities of what might be going on with Adrian. The list was endless, and she really didn't have a clue where to start, so she finally shrugged off the feeling that something was terribly wrong in Adrian's life and returned to her own little apartment.

For some odd reason, the craving for exercise was gone now and all she needed was to be close to Isabella. Needed that in a bad way.

CHAPTER FOUR

"YOU'RE up early," Caprice commented, taking a spot on the bench next to Adrian. It was quiet in the gardens this morning, and the view was breathtaking. The more she came to Costa Rica the more it felt like home to her. The stuff of tropical dreams. A yet-to-be-discovered bit of paradise still not spoilt by the outside world.

Above her, a scarlet macaw sat perched in a banana tree, casting a wary eye over the two of them, while on the dirt path at their feet a tiny leafcutter ant with a mango leaf hoisted well over its head scurried about frantically, lost from its procession. Eventually, it would catch up to its mates in the long march back to their nest, where they would munch on their leaves, turning them into gruel in which mushrooms would grow—mushrooms, their chief source of food.

A peaceful way of life, and one Caprice often thought could be of benefit to man—co-existing with what was given to them. People didn't do that so much. Especially some of the people who came into contact with one of her children. They could be intentionally cruel in ways they meant to be, and even in ways they didn't. She'd already spent a good hour this morning with one of her teenagers, Elena Gomez, trying to convince her that the next three surgeries to correct a badly misaligned jaw would be well worth the outcome. Elena couldn't see that, though. She wanted to quit. She wanted to join a convent where few would ever have to see her face, and spend her life as a recluse. She said she wanted to die because a boy she loved told her he would never love someone who looked like her.

Life in general was hurting Elena Gomez in a horrible way, and Caprice worried there was little she could do about it. There was little hope to offer right now, when Elena needed hope in a big way. This very moment! Not a year or two down the line when her surgeries would finally be finished.

"Didn't sleep much," Adrian said. "Decided to come outside and see what a Costa Rican morning looks like."

"It looks like the most beautiful morning you're every going to see," she said wistfully.

He twisted toward her, smiling. "It suits you... Costa Rica suits you."

She was surprised he would say that because she thought that it did. She liked that. Liked him saying it. Liked that he was observant that way. "I'll take that as a compliment, because I like that it does suit me. The pace is slower, the people friendlier than where I've come from, and I need that sometimes. Need someplace that makes sense, where I can spend a morning like this, and have so much beauty all to myself without the pressures of anything else closing in around me."

"Pressures, as in after your divorce?"

She blinked her surprise. "Yes. Why?"

"Because I ran away for a while after my divorce, looking for pretty much the same things you did. Looking for something that made sense."

"Where did you go?" she asked.

"Miami. A nice little abandoned, art-deco-style hotel on the beach. I liked it, stayed, bought the hotel and converted it into my house."

"And you've lived happily ever after, with everything making sense?" she asked. Normally she didn't get into personal conversations. Didn't even touch on personal topics or tidbits. But this had a good feel to it, like it was something they might have done before. And, admittedly, having an acquaintance who, for the moment, seemed more like a real friend was nice. She hadn't had that in her life for a good, long while. Hadn't trusted anyone enough to let them get that close. Not that Adrian would ever get that close. But friendship at arm's length for the next couple of weeks had a pleasant appeal to it. As long as she knew exactly what it was and kept the boundaries where they needed to be. As long as he knew that, too.

"Happily ever after?" Adrian snorted. "Hardly. I had to sell the place two years later to keep up payments to my ex-wife. That didn't make a damn bit of sense then. Still doesn't now, but that's the way it worked out."

"Yet you stayed in Miami anyway?"

"Miami's not to blame. Just my ex. And I still find my peace there. Most of the time, anyway."

"Then you're lucky. Maybe not in the way you'd originally wanted, but luckier than most. Luckier than me, actually, as I don't find much of anything in California except bad memories."

"Then why stay there?"

Caprice shrugged. "Isabella's happy there. She's close to her father…" As she still tried to keep her daughter wrapped in the delusion that her father cared for her, that was a good thing. "Also, I have my practice and a good bit of all my resources invested there. I suppose you could say that the bottom line is practicality. Living there is practical."

"But life is so short to settle only for practical, isn't it?"

"Sometimes that's the best you get. Isabella and I make it work for us. We've got each other and we're happy. That's all we need, really."

He frowned for a second, then gave a knowing shake of his head. "That's right. You're a survivor in the bad divorce wars, too."

"The worst kind of divorce. Uglier than you could ever imagine. Hurtful, bitter." It was so easy talking to Adrian, and that frightened her a little, because in the beginning it had been easy talking to Tony. Not about the deep things like feelings, but about other things…plans, details, facts. He'd listened so well, and she'd been drawn in much too easily. And now here was Adrian listening to her, and she was going beyond plans and details and facts. She was telling him personal things she'd vowed never to say to another man. The worst part was she simply didn't feel like putting up any resistance to him. None whatsoever. "He was your basic snobbish bastard who was better than everybody else, or at least that was his inflated opinion of himself, and by the time we got through it all there wasn't even a thread of civility left."

"In him, you mean."

"No, I mean in either one of us. I don't hate people, Adrian, but I truly hate that man. What he did…" She stopped. That was far enough. Adrian hadn't come out here this morning to hear her rant on about all the terrible things Tony had done. Apparently he'd had enough bad luck in the marriage area himself. "Doesn't matter," she continued. "And I didn't intend to come out here and spoil your morning with all the nitty-gritty of what went wrong in my marriage."

"Except now you've tweaked my curiosity over what could be so bad in a man that Caprice Bonaventura would hate him. You don't strike me as the type to harbor so many bad feelings, so surely you're not going to leave me dangling, are you?"

Caprice looked up as the macaw flew off, as if it didn't want to stay for the rest of the story. Smart bird. If she could have flown away with it to avoid the brutal details, she would have. "He was cruel to Isabella," she said bluntly, then stood. "He was a father who couldn't love his child as his child wasn't the picture of perfection he thought she should be. She distracted his business partners. He was embarrassed by her and he wanted to send her away to a boarding school so he wouldn't have to look at her." That was enough. Adrian knew the beginning and he could fill in the blanks all the way to the end.

"Does he ever see her now?"

"Rarely, and only for a few minutes when he does find time. Sometimes he'll stop by the house, bring in an armload of presents to assuage his guilt, then get called away before he actually has to have any interaction with his daughter."

"His loss, Caprice. Isabella's a great kid. You've done a good job raising her and she doesn't deserve that from anybody, particularly her father."

Suddenly all the animosity building in her disappeared and Caprice relaxed again. "She is a great kid, isn't she?"

"Happy, normal. Very smart. Considering everything she's had to face, she's remarkably well adjusted."

"Well adjusted, but that doesn't make up for the fact that she needs a father…a man in her life. That's why she took to you so quickly, you know. I'm afraid she sees every man as a potential father-figure for her—someone who will give her all the attention and love her own father refuses her. Right now the armload of gifts he brings distracts from her the fact that his visits are brief, and that he uses any excuse to get away as quickly as he can. But how long can that last? She is growing up and while I'm a little partial, I do think she's bright. She'll figure it out eventually, but the over-protective mother in me, and, yes, I'm admitting to being over-protective with this, would like to prevent that from happening as long as I can. Let her live with the illusion a while longer. Little girls deserve to believe that their daddies adore them."

"But children are more perceptive than we give them credit for. Perhaps she's already aware of what her father is doing, aware of his feelings."

"I've wondered about that, actually. But I still like that little bit of denial going on. Isabella deserves it, and I think I'm entitled to it, too." She smiled sadly. "And to a young child like Isabella, there's always the hope that Daddy will change his mind and accept her. I think she should have that as long as she can, because you can spend a lifetime chasing after Daddy and never, ever catch his attention or his love. So she deserves this fantasy for as long as she can hold onto it."

"Maybe so. But in the meantime, you won't allow a father-figure in because… Let me guess. In one way or another, we're all bastards." He stood, then faced her. "Your husband, probably your father…they hurt you deeply, so you hate us all."

"That's not fair!" Caprice took a step back from Adrian. He was getting too close, delving into places and feelings where he had no right to be. "On general principle I don't trust *most* of you, personally speaking anyway. But I don't hate men, if that's what you're really accusing me of. Once burned, twice shy maybe. But not hate."

He chuckled. "Sure you do, Caprice, and I understand it. I have a personal aversion to ex-wives, actually. So I do understand why you spend all your spare time trying to protect your child. What I wouldn't understand is if you didn't." He stood, then reached over and rubbed a gentle thumb at the frown line between her eyes. "It's going to be permanent there soon because you never smile, and I think you would have a beautiful smile. Isabella smiles all the time so maybe you should take a lesson from your daughter."

With that, Adrian walked away, leaving Caprice standing in the garden, speechless. At least, for a moment. Then she yelled after him, "It's none of your business, Dr McCallan." Yet he didn't turn around, as she'd expected he might.

When he disappeared through the hospital door, Caprice finally raised a finger to trace the frown line that was, indeed, beginning to find a permanent place there. She did frown too much. She knew that. But in her life there really was so little to smile about.

"He wasn't feeling well this morning," the woman said through the interpreter.

The little boy was sick. That much was apparent. Poor thing had a fever, and even without taking the boy's temperature Adrian knew it was well above normal. Probably by several degrees. He was listless, too. "When did he start feeling bad?"

"Last night. He wouldn't eat. Refused to take a drink of water. Didn't sleep well…tossed and turned. Cried off and on."

The boy was not responsive at all so far. His eyes were opened in narrow slits and staring up at Adrian, but somehow Adrian suspected they really weren't seeing very much. Or anything at all. "Miguel," he said to the four-year old child, then gave him a gentle pinch on the arm, trying to rouse him.

Miguel did flinch and moan, but not nearly enough. He should have wailed, and struggled, and kicked at Adrian. "Where did he say he hurt?"

The mother shrugged, immediately after which Miguel moaned, and his eyes fluttered open wider. The look Adrian saw there…so frightened, so confused. Would he see that same look in Sean's eyes right now? Had his son figured out that what his mother was doing was more than a casual visit? That she was using him to manipulate his father? Had he, as a father, been guilty of keeping things away from Sean that Sean had probably already guessed? The way Caprice kept things from Isabella?

As he continued to examine Miguel, Adrian thought about all the hours he'd spent on the Internet the previous night, e-mailing people who knew Sylvie, sending suggestions to Ben to pass along to the investigator they'd hired. Reading other accounts of parents who'd had children gone missing. Not that Sean was missing in a real sense. Sylvie had him and at some point she would tire of that and return him. Sean wasn't one of those children with an uncertain destiny, like so many of the lost ones out there were. In fact, his destiny was fairly certain. Bumpy for now, but safe. Yet Adrian had read so many heartbreaking stories, all the while realizing that it wasn't doing the least bit of good. Nothing he did right now would bring about results until Sylvie was ready. Which made him feel so damned helpless. It felt like he was doing nothing. Felt like he'd abandoned his son by choosing to stay in Costa Rica. But it didn't matter where he was, or what he was doing. Sylvie had her own little game to play out in her own good time.

And he did have an investigator on the job. Small comfort. But it's all he had.

So last night, as Adrian had surfed the Internet, he'd felt a little connected to the investigation, felt like he'd been doing something to help. "Has Miguel had any complaints before yesterday?" he asked. "Any aches or pains? Something you might have noticed about him that didn't seem usual?"

"No," she whispered. "He's been fine. This all came on in the evening. Very quickly. One minute he was playing with his brother, then the next he seemed sick."

Adrian nodded as he put a stethoscope to the boy's chest. Heart seemed fine. Good, steady rhythm. Strong. Lungs good, too. Dry. Nice breath sounds. No wheezing. And Miguel's belly… The little boy flinched as Adrian pressed the bell of the stethoscope to his lower belly. "That hurt?" he asked, prodding lightly over the lower right side.

Apparently it did, as Miguel did more than flinch. He let out an adult-sized howl then balled his fists and started striking out at Adrian.

Now he had the reaction he needed! "Appendicitis," Adrian said, almost under his breath. Normally, the fix was easy, a simple procedure and it was all over. Something told him this had gone beyond simple, though. In fact, he feared the worst—a burst appendix. Right at this moment the poison could be making its way through the boy's frail system, causing more than his appendix to go bad. "I'll be right back," he said to the mother, then rushed out of his cubicle, out of the mass exam room and right across the hall to Caprice's office. In spite of the fact that her door was shut, he barged in, interrupting her examination of a toddler with microtia, a congenital ear deformity where the outer ear failed to develop.

"Excuse me," Caprice protested before Adrian was all the way into the office. "I'm with a patient!" she snapped.

"So am I. Hot appendix. Probably already ruptured, or about to. Who's on call for general surgery?"

"We don't do general surgery," she said. "Refer him to the hospital."

"And how long will that take? He's been sick since last night."

Caprice thought for a moment. "You're sure about the diagnosis?"

"Belly is tender, high fever, lethargic. Even an anesthesiologist can put those symptoms together and come up with the right answer."

Caprice nodded, excused herself from the exam table and went to her desk. She dialed, listened, then argued. Then she listened and argued some more, after which she slammed the phone down. "Send him round to the emergency department. They'll look at him within the hour."

"Or he'll die within the hour, depending on the state of his appendix, if he's got gangrene, and if that gangrene's already spreading. Want to live with that on your conscience?" he snarled, taking care to keep his voice low so the child on the exam table on the other side of the room couldn't overhear them. "You've got surgical privileges here, don't you?"

"I do, but I'm not a general surgeon."

"You went through general surgery to get where you are, didn't you?"

"And I'm not sanctioned to perform general surgery here."

"So you're willing to let him wait for another hour, maybe longer, depending on how long it takes them to get set up to operate on him?" He lowered his voice even more. "It won't keep, Caprice. Trust me. This child is really sick. *He can't wait.*"

She regarded him for a moment, then nodded. "OK, I'll do it. And you'll do anesthesia," she said, then turned to the mother of the child on her exam table, said a few words in Spanish, and headed out the door. "I'll go get the OR ready, you go find Dr Makela and have him verify your opinion before we both get ourselves into trouble."

"Still don't trust me?" Adrian asked.

"Oh, I trust you *enough.* But if I'm going to put my happy existence here on the line, I've got to trust you more than enough, and so far I don't."

"You're doing the right thing," Adrian said as he headed back into the mass exam to roust Dr Makela from his exam nook.

"You'd better hope that I am, Dr McCallan. You'd better hope that I am."

Ten minutes into the surgery, the operating theater shrouded in total quiet, Caprice finally said, "You're angry because I didn't take your word, aren't you? Because I asked for a second opinion."

"Not angry. But diagnosing a hot appendix is something every first-year resident can do in his or her sleep. I knew what I was doing, *Doctor.*"

"And I'm in charge of what you're doing, *Doctor.* The decisions are mine. I question everyone, and you're no exception. That's part of my responsibility. If I don't do it, and a mistake is made, the program is in jeopardy, and I won't allow that to happen. So don't take it personally."

"Do you ever let up?" he asked. "Trust the people you ask into your program? Because, let me tell you, in the long term I wouldn't work in a situation where someone questions my judgement every step of the way. You don't win friends that way. and you certainly can't induce good doctors to return over and over that way either."

"So what you're saying is that I'm not a good doctor?" she muttered, her words coming out muffled through her mask.

"It's not about your medical skills, Caprice. It's about your need to control everything and everyone around you."

"That coming from a man I don't even trust to stay the two weeks he's committed to. The way I see it, you really don't have much room to criticize me." With that, Caprice turned her shoulder to Adrian, setting about the delicate task of cutting through the layers of tissue until the appendix was fully exposed. When she had her first peek, it was enough to tell her that Adrian had been good in his diagnosis. The appendix was hot. Reaching for a sterile sponge to clear the area of blood, she said, "And for the record, Doctor, you're an anesthesiologist. How long has it been since you've made a medical diagnosis of any sort?"

"About an hour now," he said. "And it was pretty damned good."

"I had about three months in an anesthesia rotation when I was a resident. Would you trust me to do your job? Just take my word that I could do it and let me have at it? Or would you question me? Ask somebody to look over my shoulder? Maybe pull me off the case altogether?"

"OK, maybe you have a point. I'll give you that much, but—"

"And I appreciate that. But you've got to look at this from my point of view, Adrian. I don't do anesthesiology, even though I did have a try at it for a little while years ago. You don't make medical decisions in your specialty, even though you might have had a try at general surgery years ago. Right now I've got to be careful about stepping over the line. I can't put this program at risk, even when you're sure it's appendicitis."

"So it's your policy to take another physician away from his job to check on mine?"

He was in a horrible mood now, and his horrible mood was turning into hers. Which she didn't need now that she was finally getting her first clear look at the infected organ. It was large, tenuous. Would require a steady hand or else it would rupture and the infection would start to spread through the child's body before she could even clean it out. Another ten minutes… "My policy is to always get a second opinion, no matter what the diagnosis, no matter who makes the diagnosis, including me."

"Then I apologize," he said. "In my practice I'm used to—"

"Being the boss," Caprice interrupted. "Not being bossed by women. Getting your way. Making the decisions. Want me to go on?"

Adrian smiled, his eyes crinkling above his surgical mask. "Ouch. Intentionally cruel. That hurts."

Caprice laughed. "I mean it to. You've got control issues, haven't you?"

He thought about it for a moment, then tossed her a shrug. "And you were so kind as to point that out to me. Should I thank you?" He chuckled. "Or merely grovel?"

"Groveling's good in a man, but how about I simply accept your apology?" She took up her scalpel. "And for what it's worth, you were right to push me about this. It was a good call." Then with one sure swipe she severed the appendix, removed it from Miguel's body and dropped it into the blue plastic specimen pan. "But next time I'll still get a second opinion. Keeps me happy, keeps you from future groveling."

"Anything to keep you happy," he said. "Oh, and it's not about me having a problem with a woman in charge. I think it's more that I'm set in my ways and not used to yours."

"Could have fooled me." She gave him a quick glance as she sutured the wound, and saw that he was staring at her. A stare that caused goose-bumps to shoot up her arm. Adrian was a reasonable man. A little impulsive and a little too quick to react. A little lost without his own control structure around him, she supposed. But he did listen to reason, which was good. More than that, he had genuine passion for the work. And a pair of the sexiest eyes she'd ever caught staring at her.

Blinking away the image of his eyes, Caprice refocused herself on closing the incision, wondering if Adrian truly hadn't realized he had a problem with women in charge. To be honest, that was a common condition in the medical field. Dominant male expecting subservience from the female, no matter what her position. Adrian simply seemed like the type, so maybe this was something else. Something personal. He was a good doctor otherwise. She'd give him his due and let it go.

"And so you'll know, what you said earlier about me hating men… I don't," she said, as she pulled off her surgical gown and threw it into the hamper several minutes later, after Miguel was sleeping soundly in Recovery. "I just don't have a lot of use for them in my personal life, the way you don't have a lot of use for women in charge in your professional life." She tossed him a knife-sharp smile as she dropped her surgical cap into the trash.

"And there's a difference in not hating men and not having a use for them?" he asked.

Caprice laughed. "Maybe not to the naked eye. But I know the distinctions, and that's all that matters."

"Question is, does it work for you, Caprice? Does it make you happy?"

A little while ago she would have said yes, emphatically so. Now she wasn't quite so sure. As Adrian stripped out of his scrub top and stood there bare-chested before her, her small doubts turned into great big ones. So big, in fact, she turned away lest she be caught blushing. Or staring. "Does it work for you, Adrian, always challenging a woman who's in a position of authority over you?" She tried averting her eyes, which was hard to do as even this view of him told her he was just about the best-looking man she'd ever seen, fully clothed, partially clothed, or otherwise. Or maybe she was just starved for something she hadn't thought about in ages.

"I'm not denying anything. I have a huge problem with women trying to control me. Some women, some areas of my life. I don't think it extends into my professional life, but that's only one man's opinion—the woman in charge of him thinks otherwise. Guess it remains to be seen, doesn't it?"

"Then I'd say we both have some problems to deal with," she returned.

"Who says I want to deal with mine? And who even says it's a problem?"

That surprised her, coming from him, Yet, in a way, it didn't. The more she knew about Adrian the more she wondered if anyone could ever *really* know a man like him. In some ways he scared her, in some ways he intrigued her, and in more ways than she wanted to admit he attracted her like no man ever had. Which took her right back to the ways he scared her. "Look, Adrian, I meant to keep this professional between us, but it seems to be getting off course. That's my fault. I shouldn't have let it happen…"

"Maybe you wanted it to happen," he said, as he pulled on a fresh scrub top. "Maybe you're tired of keeping up so many walls around you and Isabella, and you were ready for someone who doesn't abide walls."

"What's Isabella got to do with this?" she snapped, annoyed that he was making sense. Too much sense.

"Everything, as far as I can see. You're the textbook self-sacrificing mother, aren't you? A martyr to motherhood. Everything for your daughter and nothing for yourself, all because a man did wrong by both of you?"

"How dare you?"

"See, there you go, getting riled. And I didn't mean it as anything derogatory, Caprice. But you always take it that way. You bristle when you don't need to. I saw it the first time I met you, and had my first look at Isabella. You were ready to have a go at my throat then, weren't you? One look at your child that you couldn't interpret and Caprice, *the mother*, went on the defensive. And she's on the defensive again because she's afraid of what's going on with us, which really isn't anything like any friendship I've ever had. To be honest, I don't know if you want to be friends or want to take me on as a sparring partner. A stand-in to bash in place of your ex-husband? Someone you can sling a few barbs at…barbs left over from your divorce?"

"Aren't you a great one to stand there and criticize me?" she snorted. "You, with all this hostility built up over a woman who has the power to order you about. You know you're that way and don't even care."

"Maybe I've earned my attitude," he said.

"And maybe I've earned mine," she defended, caught somewhere between anger and sadness, as everything he said was true. "You don't know what it's like, Adrian."

"To get divorced? I sure as hell do. To absolutely hate your ex? I'm right there with you on that one, too."

"To want to protect a child so badly that you lose reason." Her voice quivered with tears. "I'm guilty of that, Adrian. I'll admit it, and not apologize for it. I've been doing it an awfully long time and sometimes I do strike out at the wrong people. I know that, too, and I'm sorry I seem to be striking out at you. But…" She shut her eyes to fight back the tears. "But you're the first person… first man…I've really wanted to get to know since… since I can't remember when. And that scares me since I'm not really looking for a relationship of any sort with anyone. Yet here you are."

Adrian crooked his finger under Caprice's chin and tilted her face to his. "You're quite the fighter, Caprice. I think that's probably a good thing. To do what you do you have to be strong, and I admire that."

"Do you really, or am I just another woman in charge you're more compelled to argue with?"

"Some arguments come with good things. Depends on who's doing the arguing. And I do understand what you're up against more than you know," he said gently, then, as if he'd been stung by a wasp, he pulled away. "Look, I have a line of patients waiting to see me," he said gruffly, then strode away, leaving Caprice to wonder what had just happened between them. Friendship? Something more? Something much, much less?

"I should stick to my policy," she muttered, following Adrian out the door and taking the long way back to her office so she wouldn't bump into him in the hall.

Damn, he'd wanted to kiss her. Another five seconds, and that's exactly what would have happened. A nice circumspect kiss, perhaps? Or something much more? And it wouldn't have been the knight in shining armor riding in to kiss the damsel in distress. He wanted Caprice. Through all the ups and downs and mood swings in their brief relationship, there was something about her that pulled him in like no other woman had. Which was what scared him. Caprice had all the issues going on in her he didn't want to deal with. They were right there on her sleeve, easy to see, ready to jump out and bite, and yet he was still being pulled, and doing precious little to stop it.

She had been right about it, though, when she'd accused him of having a problem with women who were in a position to control his life. He did! Although he'd never thought of it that way. Sylvie was the ultimate in control and he wasn't about to mess himself up with anyone else like her. While Caprice wasn't at all like Sylvie, she did control her own daughter rigidly, even if only to protect her. And she had so many other issues…ones he already knew, ones he didn't.

"And here I am, going right in there for more," he muttered. Oh, it would be easy to avoid Caprice, keep it strictly professional, and maybe he should. Hell, who was he kidding here? He *absolutely* should! Yet this morning, when he'd asked one of the surgical techs where Caprice was, and he'd learnt she always took her morning coffee out in the garden, what had he done? Like an idiot, he'd gone there to wait for her. Then just now, with that stupid little stunt…the kiss that had come so close… What was he thinking? There were too many other complications going on in his life, yanking him in other directions. His work. Most of all his missing son.

He didn't need Caprice. Didn't need her issues.

But, dear God, he did want her.

CHAPTER FIVE

"A HOUSE call?" Adrian asked through a yawn. "You want me to go out with you on a house call?"

"A house call," Caprice confirmed, fighting to avert her eyes from Adrian. He'd plodded to the door to let her in, a sheet wrapped around his waist, and now he was back on the bed, same condition, and she noticed every little bit of him that was showing, and imagined a few bits that weren't. She may have sworn off men in her life, but she was still human after all. Liked to look. Especially liked to look at the tousled look of him…unkempt hair, shadow of a beard, eyes barely opened. Bedroom eyes not quite awake yet. Utterly sexy. Utterly off limits.

Briefly, she wondered if he might be naked under the sheet, but before that thought got out of hand, and before he could see the faint blush rising in her cheeks, she turned to the window in his tiny room and forced every last speck of concentration she had on the hard, asphalt parking lot outside.

By design, he'd gotten the room with the worst view. She'd assigned it to him in one of those first moments when she'd still hated him. Well, perhaps "hate" was too strong a word. She'd assigned it to him in one of those first moments when she hadn't been particularly fond of him. Times were changing, though. So were her feelings, as she was definitely fond of him now. In the carnal sense, anyway. That was a part of her she'd still admit, although not give in to. Not for a very long time on that account. If ever again.

"She left some time early last night, the nurse told me. I'd scheduled her for tests this morning, and some counseling as she's having such a rough time of this the older she gets, and had her on the surgical schedule first up tomorrow." Elena Gomez had disappeared in the night. Normally she would have simply scheduled another child into her place, but Elena was special to Caprice. Her age, her fears…that far-away stare she saw in Elena's eyes every time she looked at her, a stare she knew so well. It all took its toll on Caprice, crept in and haunted her, caused her concern for Elena to involve her in ways she tried not to involve herself with her patients. But there were so many reminders… "I'm sure she's gone back to her village, and I want to go after her and convince her to return here."

Adrian reached up to run his hand through his hair and his sheet dropped precariously low over his stomach, yet he did nothing to retrieve it. "So what do we do about clinic today?"

"We work harder when get back this afternoon, and make up for lost time." Practical answer. Not a good one because they couldn't have the day off. There were too many patients to see, too many surgical preps and tests to get under way. But it was the best she could offer. "We'll stay on later tonight if we have to, until everything is finished."

Adrian thought about that for a moment, then frowned. "So why are you going after her?" he asked, still making no move to cover himself. "Is that typical of you?"

"No," she said stiffly, catching the sight of him from the corner of her eye. "It's not. But Elena is…she's a struggling teenager. We're so close to the end of her surgeries, all little things to do to get her to the end now, and she wants to give up."

"But you don't want her to give up," he said. "And it's personal, as you're willing to break your schedule, and mine, to go after her."

"No, I don't want to give up," she replied, still fighting to keep her voice stiff and unaffected. "And I don't want her giving up. She's been so brave—"

"Ten minutes," he interrupted. "Give me time to shower and grab a cup of coffee."

"You'll come?" she asked, surprised how much she wanted him to. She could have made the journey herself, of course. Elena lived only thirty kilometers away. The road wasn't bad as dirt roads went. The jungle between here and there not too wild. An easy trip, all in all. Yet when she'd learnt that Elena had gone, the first thing that had come to mind had been that she wanted Adrian to go with her to find the girl. It wasn't a rational thought. More like it was a buffer to fend off the queasy feeling in the pit of her stomach. A girl that age so distraught emotionally…she could do so many things, none of them good. Caprice couldn't, *wouldn't* think any further than that. The two of them would go after Elena and bring her back to Dulce. That's all there was to it.

"Of course I'll come," he said. Starting to pull off the bed sheet, Adrian took a look down and had a second thought about it.

Caprice turned fully to face him. "I'm not always nice to you, Adrian, and I'm sorry about that. I have my ups and downs with this operation, I'll admit it. I'm the first one to admit that I do get emotionally involved. Probably more so than I should, as you're seeing with Elena. But I'm grateful to you for doing this. Elena means a lot to me, and I'm scared for her. She wavers emotionally."

"That's why you're good at what you do," he said, his voice oddly gentle. "Because you do get so emotionally involved. I know it's not the image of yourself you want to put out, but it's a good thing, Caprice. Don't ever apologize for it. Now…" He gave his eyebrows a playful wiggle. "Sheet's coming off in five seconds. Your choice—stay or leave."

Caprice took the hint and scurried out of the room. Not that she was a prude. At another time she might have called Adrian's bluff and stayed for the so-called unveiling. But not now. Not with Isabella down the hall. Not in the middle of a medical mission. Not when she was so frightened for Elena.

And most especially not when she was so attracted to Adrian.

"It's been too long," Adrian snapped into the payphone in the hall. "We should have had him back by now, or at least have heard something from Sylvie. I'm coming back." No word from Sylvie, meaning no word about Sean. The investigator had turned up absolutely nothing yet, and while Adrian still wasn't worried about his son's well-being, he was getting really angry now. Ready to throttle his ex-wife.

"That's not going to help matters, Adrian," Ben said through the crackling connection. Words were cutting in and out, and the volume alternately rose and fell so it either sounded like shouting from the other end or whispering. "Like I told you, she's playing her game. If you come home now, she wins. And in your mood… I want you level-headed when we go up against her."

"Level-headed?" Adrian snarled. He glanced at his watch. Caprice was waiting. "Tell me what in this situation I've got to be level-headed about?"

"Look, I know it's frustrating. But I've been dealing with Sylvie for years and you and I both know it's all a matter of waiting until she makes her demand in her own good time. She wants to get you riled, Adrian. Wants you damned good and angry, which is exactly what's happening now. And every time you do get riled to this point, she gets more out of you."

That much was true. Sylvie knew exactly which of his buttons to push, and how hard to push them. "Draw up the custody papers, Ben. When she finally plays her hand, I want a hand to play myself. I'm not going through this again. Sean's old enough to understand now…" *something he'd realized watching the relationship between Caprice and Isabella* "…and I'll have to explain it to him." Old enough now…so many years of protecting his little boy from a mother who had no idea what it was like to protect a child. A lump formed in Adrian's throat. Sean was old enough now to see, to understand what was going on between his parents, which put Sylvie's antics on a whole different level.

Facing the truth with his son…it wasn't going to be easy. It wouldn't be easy for Caprice and Isabella either. But a word that was rarely ever associated with parenting was stabbing at him right now—respect. He loved, he protected and he respected his son. A large part of that respect was honesty, and allowing the lies about Sylvie to continue was not giving Sean the respect he was due. He smiled, thinking about Isabella coming to terms with the word "respect", then thought about Caprice coming to terms with the concept. It wasn't going to be easy. But it was going to be necessary for them, too. And soon. "I'm not putting this off any longer," he said to Ben. "And I'll take my chances, however it turns out."

"I've got them drawn up and ready to file when the time's right, actually. I knew you'd come around at some point, and I drew them up a while ago. They're already in your file, waiting."

"Do you think the court will give me full custody and revoke her rights? And be honest with me here, Ben. I know we've talked about this before, but Sylvie's never gone as far as she has this time, and I'm hoping that the judge will see what she's doing in terms of the emotional damage she could cause Sean. Not to mention the fact that she doesn't have the legal right to take him away like this."

He wanted full custody more than he'd wanted anything else in life, but he'd never truly believed that would happen. Not even having spent all these years being the one to raise Sean. The simple fact of the matter was that Sean shared his blood with Sylvie, not with him. Courts always took that into consideration, whether or not it should be considered. Sylvie had never been

Sean's mother in any way that counted, didn't want to be Sean's mother in any way that mattered, and she only put on the pretense when she wanted more money. Everyone saw that, but Adrian didn't trust the court to see it that way since it had granted Sylvie partial custody with stipulations even when she'd specifically told the court she didn't want it.

That, before she'd figured out a way to manipulate him into paying her. That little deal had come later, when she'd seen how devoted to the boy he was. Sylvie, true to form, hadn't missed a beat on that discovery. She asked him for money, said it would keep her from returning to court for a modification of the custody agreement. An implied threat he'd recognized for what it had been. Pay her and let the status quo remain. Don't pay her and the rest of it was a great big question.

Adrian's fear in refusing Sylvie had always been that bringing this situation with her to the legal system might end with him being denied all parental rights. Now, though, he didn't have a choice, and the worry of losing Sean plagued him.

"I'm not making any promises here, Adrian, but I think the court will take this latest stunt of hers under strict advisement," Ben returned. "Fact is, she doesn't have the right to do this. The custody terms are laid out and she's gone against them."

"Another fact is she's his mother," Adrian snapped.

"And you're his father."

"On a piece of paper only." Legally, he was. Sean had been born of a marriage union, and bore his name, and the law made Sean his son. But the law allowed Sylvie to continue to be his mother, and that was the problem. Anything else he simply didn't trust.

"Legalities don't make a father, Adrian. You're his father. Sean knows that. So does Sylvie. If you want my opinion, she's making her last grand stand because Sean is getting old enough to see her for what she is. I think it's a last act of desperation before Sean can go to the court himself and testify how his mother uses him.

I know you'd never allow him into court to do that, but Sylvie's not like you and she sees using Sean that way as a parental right. It's probably never crossed her mind that you wouldn't allow him to testify because she wouldn't have a problem doing that herself. So she's decided to get everything she can, while she can."

"Well, whatever she's thinking or plotting, I want him back, Ben. That's all I care about. She can have every last cent of mine if that's what it takes, but I want him safe, and I don't want him emotionally upset over this. When I'm convinced he's fine, we're going to do it this time. I swear, we're going after a custody change."

"I hope so, Adrian. For the boy's sake, and for yours, I really hope so."

"You make sure those papers are ready to file when I give you the OK." Sighing, Adrian hung up and looked out of the window across the hall. Caprice was leaning against an old truck, talking to Isabella. In a way he envied her, having her child all to herself. No fights with the other parent. It's what he wanted…having Sean to himself, having Sylvie completely out of the picture. Having some peace in their lives without the worry of it being disrupted. Sean needed that. So did he.

Yes, it was time to do just that, and hope for the best. Separating a child from his mother permanently wasn't an easy thing to do, unless the mother was Sylvie. Perhaps, to be fair, he would see about allowing chaperoned visitation through the court if she truly did want to visit her son from time to time. He doubted she would, though. But it was an option to consider, even though she didn't deserve Sean.

Adrian opened the door and started out into the parking lot. Caprice and Isabella were tossing a stuffed animal back and forth to each other, laughing, smiling, having such a lovely time. Yes, he did envy Caprice. She had with her daughter what he wanted with his son, and wasn't sure he would ever have.

* * *

"Isabella didn't want to come with us," Caprice said, settling into the driver's side of the old truck they were borrowing from one of the plantation owners. "Why go along with her mother on a boring old medical visit when she's made so many friends here…children who keep coming back for more surgeries? So many children to play with. I think she's comfortable because no one here makes fun of her."

"Children can be cruel," Adrian said, looking for a seat belt, which wasn't to be found.

"So can adults. Some mean to, some don't. But children are perceptive. They know. They see the subtle expressions, hear the whispers. And it's so much worse coming from an adult, because adults should know better. Children look up to them, expect them to be better. But they can be just as cruel as children."

"Which is why you're giving up half a day to go chasing after Elena Gomez, isn't it? Because people have been cruel to her."

Caprice nodded. "She's had her share of ridicule. Some children eventually toughen to it, but Elena's fifteen, and she never has. She takes it to heart and it hurts her so deeply. And now she wants a boy who doesn't want her. It's all so hard to take when you're that age, even without Elena's problems. But if you're that age and going through all the surgeries to correct a deformed jaw…" She shook her head. "People *are* cruel."

"So you're off to her rescue." He reached over and gave her hand a gentle squeeze. "I think I mentioned this earlier, but you're a good doctor, Caprice. And a good mother. Isabella and Elena are both lucky to have you in their lives. So, tell me about Elena. What's her prognosis?"

"Quite good, actually. Three surgeries and I think we'll be through. Eventually, she'll have to go through some orthodontia to bring her teeth into line with her jaw, and maybe some contouring to her cheeks, but she's doing brilliantly, actually. In fact, I was hoping that this surgery might be the last of her major procedures, then the next trip out let the dentists take over. After that, some tweaking and adjustments."

"Over how long a period?"

"Eighteen months, optimistically. A lot of it depending on her healing time, as well as my schedule. So, at the longest, two years."

"Such a long time in a young woman's life," Adrian commented sympathetically.

"Too long. Which is the problem. At fifteen, that's a lifetime. Everything is about right now. It's urgent, it's a crisis. Tomorrow doesn't count when everything is about today."

"But it's a lifetime with hope that she wouldn't have without you. Don't forget that."

Forgetting was one thing she never did. Never would do. "Do you mind if we make a couple of quick stops on the way?" she asked, changing the subject.

"You don't take a compliment too well, do you?" he asked, settling back into his seat as they left the little town of Golfito and headed south along the bumpy road.

"I don't need compliments," she replied, stiffly. "I do my job, I do it well, that's all there is to it."

Instead of pursuing it any further, Adrian slid down a little, laid his head back against the seat, and shut his eyes. For which she was glad because he was correct. She didn't take compliments very well. Didn't want them. Didn't deserve them. Shouldn't have jumped down his throat about it, though. Apologies later, she decided. Where Adrian was concerned, there would probably be one or two more to make by then, anyway.

Twenty minutes of heavy silence had passed when they finally came to the tiny village of Santa Clara. It was a beautiful farming area…coffee, sugar cane, bananas, oranges. And the farms were all small here, unlike so many that had, over time, turned into large company ranches. In a way this area was still pristine, untouched. Lush tropical jungle stretched right out to the white, sandy beaches, while small, isolated islands dotted the coastline, connected only by tenuous sand spits. Above, there were cliffs that in some areas shaded the waters for part of the day. Swimming in a shaded ocean… Caprice had always vowed she would take time to do that one day. Perhaps bring Isabella here and teach her how to snorkel, or maybe they would borrow horses from one of the farms to go for a ride. "I have a stop here," she said, finally breaking the silence. "Luis Diego Soto. Hemangioma removed, post-operative one year." A non-malignant tumor.

"Where?" Adrian asked, his eyes still closed.

"Lip. Last time I checked it was healing nicely, but…"

"But the mama bird can't bring herself to let the little ones fly away from the nest."

Caprice smiled. "Something like that, I suppose. So, do you ever go back and check?"

"Sometimes. But in my specialty you don't get as involved. You meet them, explain the procedure to the parents, then the next time you see your patient you put him, or her, to sleep, maintain them through the surgery, and check on them once or twice when they're coming round after it's over. It's not the same as following a patient over a long term."

"By design?"

"What? My avoidance of interaction or personal relationships evident in the type of specialty I chose?" He laughed. "Nothing as complicated as that. I like the technical edge to anesthesiology—working with the gases and machines. Liked it the first time I rotated through, back when I was in med school, and nothing changed after I'd spent time in all the other various specialties."

Caprice laughed, too. "And you don't have to keep horrible hours like the rest of us."

He finally opened his eyes, then turned sideways to grin at her. "Well, there is that."

"All those evenings without a commitment. I'd ask you what

you do with yourself, but we're here." And she didn't want to know. Truth was, she didn't want to picture Adrian with any kind of a social or personal life. He was too attractive to be alone, to be without a woman. Men like him never were without, and she simply didn't want to find out what kind of woman filled his evenings or his bed. "And, I'm sorry, Adrian."

"About what?"

"Not being polite when you were complimenting me. You're right. I don't take compliments well. I snapped at you, and I shouldn't have."

"Accepted."

She laughed. "Do you suppose I could bank a couple of future apologies with you? Seems like I'm always in need of one."

"Consider them banked. And at the risk of using one of them right away, you're under a lot of stress here." A wicked grin slid easily to his lips. "I understand, and, all things considered, you're really not as bad as you could be."

"I'm not as bad as I could be?" She raised an amused eyebrow. "Are you purposely trying to provoke me into something here, Doctor?"

"You're sexy when provoked. Looks good on you."

"So this would be the place where I protest, probably say something I'll later regret, then use up one of those apologies? This is where I'll get all provoked over you thinking I'm sexy when I'm provoked, which will fuel your desire to observe me being sexy while fueling mine to be provoked, as I do get provoked a lot? Is that what you're implying?"

Adrian chuckled. "Something like that. Mutual gratification of sorts. I get mine, you get yours."

"Well, calm down, Doctor. I'm not getting provoked, and I'm actually flattered that you think I'm sexy when provoked. How's that for something you didn't expect?"

"He was a damn idiot."

"Who?"

"Your husband, for letting you get away."

"You're right, he was. But for other reasons. I appreciate the compliment, though. Appreciate the fact that a woman with so many *issues* can still be sexy to a man who loathes women with issues. I haven't thought of myself as sexy in a very long time."

"Well, trust me. I've made up for the drought."

"But only when I'm provoked?" she asked.

Adrian withheld his answer as Caprice came to stop in front of a white-frame house. Small, square like a box, with a over-hanging porch, it sat amid a clump of banana trees that concealed most if it. In fact, without a good look off to the side of the road, the house might have gone unnoticed. "Want to come in with me?" she asked, a little sad that the pleasant banter between them had come to an end. "We won't be here long," she continued, grabbing a canvas sack of medical supplies out from behind the seat then hopping down to the ground.

"They won't find it too intrusive, me coming inside with you?"

"People here are not like the people back home. They *want* you to be intrusive. It's considered being friendly."

"That said by the woman who doesn't want personal involvement," he replied, stepping out of the truck.

"You're not going to get me provoked, Adrian. At least, not right now." She laughed as she climbed up the steps to the front door, then knocked.

"Ah, the promise of later," he countered, whispering in her ear as Maria Gabriella Soto opened the door and invited them in.

The stop was brief. Caprice did a quick check of Luis's lip, turned down the offer of a mid-morning snack, and they were back on the road within fifteen minutes.

"Nice work," Adrian commented, settling back into the passenger's seat. "Barely a scar."

"It was pretty vascular. Lots of blood supply to the tumor, and the skin was paper thin. Sometimes when you get into those procedures you don't know how it will turn out."

"It turned out happy," Adrian said.

"Happy?"

"Did you see the look on Luis's face? He was happy."

"I suppose I never thought of it like that…that my surgery turned out happy. But it did, didn't it?"

"Isn't that always the ultimate outcome? To make someone happy?"

"And increase quality of life."

"Which translates into happy," Adrian insisted.

"Better watch yourself, Adrian. You're almost sounding like an optimist."

"Better watch yourself, Caprice. You're on the verge of getting personal. That could be just as sexy as you being provoked."

The rest of the ride to the next stop was done in silence, but this time the silence between them was anything but heavy. After a quick stop to check Daniel Escalante's suture line from previous surgery for craniosynostosis, a condition where the joints in the skull close prematurely in an infant, they finally arrived at the Gomez house, a friendly little pink cottage with a goat in the front yard.

No one seemed at home as they approached the front door, and after Caprice knocked for a third time, a tiny, weathered woman ventured to peek out the curtains at them.

"Mrs Gomez," Caprice whispered, stepping back to make sure the woman could see her. "She's shy. Didn't want to ask for help with Elena. Just told her to hang her head down so people wouldn't notice too much."

"And Elena's father?"

Caprice shrugged. "No one has said anything about him, and I've never asked. As far as I know, it's just Elena and her mother." Secretly, she wondered if Elena's father had been like

Tony—appalled by his own daughter. Or like her own father, for that matter.

"She's gone to bed," Mrs Gomez said through the screen door. Mrs Gomez, dressed in black, was barely distinguishable from the dark background of the house interior behind her. "She said she's tired. She wants to be left alone." The words came in broken English, and the tone of Mrs Gomez's voice was as broken.

"Could I see her?" Caprice asked.

Mrs Gomez cast a wary glance to Adrian and pulled a black shawl from her shoulders up around her head.

"This is my…my partner, Dr McCallan. He helps me with the surgery," Caprice explained.

Mrs Gomez studied Adrian for a moment, then inclined her head. "She wants to be alone," she repeated. "No visitors. Please, go away."

So much shame in something that wasn't shameful. Caprice thought. Tony had turned people away so they wouldn't have to see Isabella, but that had been because he had been embarrassed. Mrs Gomez was only trying to protect her daughter, submit to her daughter's wishes, and Caprice understood that. Her heart went out to the woman. So many people suffered in a situation like this. "Just for a minute. I want to tell her she can come back any time."

The woman ventured a quick, hopeful glance at Caprice, then nodded. "For a minute." She stepped back as Caprice opened the screen door and stepped inside, but wedged herself in the doorway before Adrian could enter. It wasn't an inhospitable act as much as a shielding one, because she did gesture for him to take a seat in an old wooden rocker on the porch before she closed the screen door on him.

Inside, Caprice made her way through the dark hallway to the bedroom on the left. She'd been here before, seen the homey attempt with the sparse furnishings—a few scattered chairs, a table, a shelf with books, a floor lamp topped with a tattered shade. Mrs

Gomez had taken odd jobs to support herself and Elena—sewing, weaving, gardening and selling produce and fruit—and this house was a fitting tribute to the woman's devotion to keeping her small family together. In remote areas such as this, women often didn't have an opportunity to make their own way in the world. Their recourse was to marry, or go to the convent to join the sisters.

Caprice admired what Mrs Gomez had done, and all for the love of a daughter who, like Isabella, had a father who didn't want her. "Elena," she called, as she tapped on the bedroom door. "It's Dr Bonaventura. Could I come in for a moment?"

No response, but she didn't expect one.

"Elena. Just for a moment, please. I want to discuss your next surgery."

Still not a sound from inside.

"Elena, I understand why you left. It's frightening, and I know you've been through so many of these things before." She understood more than anyone could know. "But I want to talk about it for a minute or two." She pressed her ear to the door, fully expecting to hear sobbing or the fits of a temper tantrum, but inside there wasn't a sound. Suddenly, the warning hairs stood up on the back of her neck. "Dear God, no," she choked, pushing the door open. But it wouldn't budge. Something heavy was obstructing it. "Adrian!" she screamed, shoving all her weight against the door, succeeding to move what was on the other side but a few inches. "Adrian, please, help me!" she screamed again at the tops of her lungs.

Caprice took another shove at the door and the solid object on the other side budged again. By the time she was braced for a third go at it, Adrian was at her side. "She's committing suicide," Caprice gasped. "Door's blocked. Can't get in."

"Damn," he grunted, immediately throwing his own weight at the door. It opened all the way, with the heavy bureau on the other side scraping slowly across the wooden floorboards.

Before Adrian had time to right himself, Caprice scooted around him and ran into the room, then paused halfway to the bed. Elena was sitting in the middle, cross-legged, agitated, her face drained of color, her breathing shallow and rapid. In her hands she was clutching an empty bottle of some sort.

Immediately Caprice lunged for the bottle and grabbed it out of Elena's fidgety hands. "Aspirin," she said to Adrian, fighting back the nausea trying to rise in her. Contrary to what most people thought, aspirin wasn't harmless, and an overdose could cause convulsions, stop breathing, bring on death. Those were only a few of the horrible consequences of an overdose.

Adrian ran to the opposite side of the bed, immediately bending to feel for a pulse in Elena's neck.

"Elena," Caprice said, grabbing a penlight from her medical bag, clicking it on and shining it in the girl's eyes.

"Fast, thready," Adrian said of the girl's pulse rate. Typical of an aspirin overdose. She was probably also close to dangerously low blood pressure, which turned out to be the case as Adrian checked that next.

"Responsive, sluggish," Caprice responded, referring to the action of her pupils. "Elena, can you hear me?"

No response, even though Elena was getting more and more fidgety—a side-effect of the drug's toxicity. She was moving, jerking around on the bed, yet she was on the verge of collapse, even unconsciousness.

"I don't have anything to take care of this," Caprice choked. Contrary to popular thought, ingested poisons were not always best vomited out. In the case of aspirin, it could be so corrosive it might cause internal bleeding. In a place where there was no means to control it, it could prove fatal. What they needed here was charcoal. Good, old charcoal used to start a fire would bind to the poison and keep it from spreading. But they didn't have charcoal.

Elena's head fell to the side and Adrian immediately propped her back up and gave her a good shake. "Stay awake!" he demanded, his voice sharp enough to cut through her drowsiness. "Do you hear me, Elena? You've got to stay awake!"

The girl responded to him in a slow, deliberate blink but nothing else. "Do you know how many pills she took?" Caprice called to Mrs Gomez, who huddled outside in the hall, weeping. She looked confused, scared. Her basic understanding of English had totally vanished, and what she said to Caprice in Spanish was too fast and garbled to be understood.

"Bottle looks new," Adrian said, taking a quick look at the label. "No wear and tear on the paper label."

"Then it could have been full." She looked over at Mrs Gomez again, holding up the bottle. "How much?" she cried. "I need to know, how much?"

Elena's mother stared for a moment, then held up her fingers in a measure that indicated the bottle might have been about three-quarters full. That was a lot of pills to ingest, and that knowledge arced back and forth between Caprice and Adrian.

"Is there a hospital anywhere near here?" he asked.

Caprice shook her head. "There's a mission house a few kilometers away, with a small medical clinic. Doctor's in twice a week, but I don't know… He would have some basic supplies, though. I know he stocks up at Dulce."

"Only other choice is to fly her out and I don't think we've got time to get the plane here and get her back."

Grim words, but what Adrian said was the truth. Elena was dying now. They had no way to treat her effectively here, and no way to get her out before her condition deteriorated fatally. It was the mission clinic or nothing, "You carry her out," she said, jumping off the bed and running for the door. "I'll drive."

She barely spoke as she ran past Mrs Gomez. Offering a word or two to let her know they were going to the clinic,

Caprice was out the door with Adrian on her heels, Elena in his arms, in mere seconds.

This couldn't be happening, she thought as the truck sped forward down the bumpy road. Not again!

Stethoscope still in his ears as he kept up his assessment on the road, Adrian looked at Elena's face for the first time. A beautiful face. An amazing work in progress. A testament to the way Caprice cared for these children. She was right. Elena had been so close to the end of her medical journey. Her face was nearly a completed work. Couldn't she have seen that when she looked in the mirror? Couldn't see have seen that when she'd made the decision to take her own life?

Just one look, Elena, he thought as he listened to her heart beating more and more weakly, the life in it ebbing. *Just one look.* "I'm sorry," he whispered, looking over at Caprice. Her face was caught in the same expression of disbelief it had been mere minutes ago when they'd pushed through the door and discovered what Elena had done. For someone who vowed not to take it personally, this was very personal to Caprice. "I'm so sorry. I know you really care about her."

"Apparently not enough," she said, her voice thin and sharp.

"It's not your fault," he said. "You've done everything you were suppose to, but we can't always predict the outcomes."

"Can't we?" she snapped. Angry tears streaked down her cheeks as she swerved to avoid an old man on a bicycle taking up a little more road than he ought to. "I knew how badly she's been hurt, and I didn't do anything about it."

"You gave her a chance, sweetheart. You've done everything that's humanly possibly to make her life better."

"No," she whispered. "Don't you understand? I didn't do anything. Nothing! I've always known this could be the outcome, but I…" She let go of the steering-wheel with one hand long enough to swipe at her tears then gripped the steering-wheel again with such force that her knuckles went white. "I didn't do anything to stop it. She's my responsibility, but I didn't do enough."

"She isn't only *your* responsibility, Caprice. There are other people in her life."

"Other people who don't love her enough, other people who've shunned her, other people who've denied her because they're embarrassed. No, Adrian. She's my responsibility and I've failed her."

Adrian reached over, giving Caprice's shoulder a gentle squeeze. "For once in your life let somebody else be strong for you," he whispered. "Let somebody in who wants to help you."

"You just don't understand," she said, giving way to tears again. "Nobody can."

"Because of Isabella?" he asked. "Is that what this is about? Because she's a strong little girl. You've given her an amazing sense of self-worth."

"Not Isabella. It's about Carlina, my sister. She killed herself when she was Elena's age."

CHAPTER SIX

THE clinic was locked up tight, but the monk who lived at the tiny wayside mission didn't object when Adrian offered to break in. In fact, Brother Flavian took a kick or two at the thick wooden door himself in an attempt to get it open. It was Adrian's kick that did it, though. Broke it right down to the hinges, and left it gaping.

Inside, without a word, as if they anticipated each other's movements, Adrian went straight to the exam table in the small office, laid Elena down on it and took her vital signs while Caprice started rummaging through the meager supplies on the shelf in the room, looking for a lavage tube—the tube to be inserted through Elena's nose into her stomach, commonly called an NG tube or nasogastric tube. She wasn't sure what she'd find, and the tube she eventually came up with was an unexpected surprise. "I think this will do," she said, even though it was infant-sized.

The activated charcoal Adrian produced, with the assistance of Brother Flavian, who'd done a brilliant job of breaking into the medicine supply without causing permanent damage to the cabinet lock, was a good bit of fortune, too. "What else?" the monk asked, as he looked over at Elena, who seemed in great distress.

Her breathing was decreasing. So was her blood pressure, Adrian guessed, without taking another reading right at that moment. Her agitation was spiraling down, too, almost to the point she was totally without movement. Not a good sign, though. It meant the poison was overtaking her and, in effect, shutting her down.

"Oxygen?" Adrian asked Brother Flavian. He was a portly, older man who'd long since given up the long brown robes for baggy khaki pants and a loose-fitting floral shirt. Much more practical in the jungle.

"Might have a tank of it here somewhere," he said, scurrying out of the room to have a look.

As Caprice busied herself inserting an intravenous line, Adrian, in a swift, precise movement, inserted the NG tube into Elena, listened with the stethoscope to make sure it was in her stomach, then took the large-bore syringe Caprice had previously filled with the liquefied activated charcoal and forced it down the tube.

Elena's slender body immediately stiffened, and reflexively started to fight the procedure by twisting and turning.

"I'll go find something to calm her down," Caprice said, on her way out the door once Adrian's procedure was under way. "Maybe we'll get lucky and there will be some Valium here."

"See if there's something to get her metabolic acidosis under control, too," Adrian said, not quite so hopeful on that front. By now the acid levels in Elena's body were on the rise because of the aspirin, risking a stomach or intestinal bleed, and they needed to normalize that situation as much as possible. But to have the proper drugs in a tiny clinic such as this? He wasn't holding his breath on that one.

Caprice gave him a quick nod, her face showing the strain. "They could have some sodium bicarb," she said, even though she didn't sound confident about it.

As she ran out the door, Adrian commenced the second round of charcoal down the tube. It went down in dribs and drabs, provoking the same reaction from the girl, only this time she bucked harder than before, her entire body thrashing about in the bed. "I need a hand in here," Adrian called, fighting to hold Elena down and trying to stop her from injuring herself and at the same time trying to keep the NG tube in place. He feared the IV might also be torn out if they didn't get her calmed down soon.

"Right here," Brother Flavian said, running into the room, pulling an oxygen cylinder on its stand behind him. "What can I do?"

"Hold her down while I get some restraints." Simple procedure. Normally, he was against tying a patient to the bed, only for this one's sake he had to do it. So while Brother Flavian took over holding Elena down, Adrian turned away to find gauze rolls or any other soft material suitable for tying her down.

"She's struggling worse," the monk said, as Adrian stretched to the top shelf. "I don't think... Dear God, I didn't mean..."

Adrian spun around in time to see the NG tube become dislodged from Elena and fall to the side of the bed. Much better that than the IV, but poor Brother Flavian looked almost as stricken as Elena.

"I'm sorry," he mumbled, his face going beet red. "I don't know how it happened."

"Easy fix," Adrian assured him, grabbing a new tube from the supplies. "Just keep her steady for another few seconds and..." As he grabbed the tube, the liquid charcoal he'd just forced down Elena started bubbling from her mouth, then her arm started twitching. By the time Adrian had taken two giants steps toward the bed, the twitch had extended up her arm and she'd drawn her hand to her chest as her hand contorted into a clawlike fist. And more charcoal dribbled from her mouth.

"She's seizing," he shouted to Caprice, "and probably aspirating the charcoal." In other words, the seizure was causing Elena to regurgitate the charcoal and as it was coming up it was in danger of getting sucked down into her lungs. A dreadful, deadly situation.

"I'm sorry," the monk wailed, backing himself into a corner when Caprice came running in.

"I need to intubate," Adrian shouted, ignoring the monk.

Caprice was already on top of that, because as Adrian shouted the command she was searching for the laryngoscope and an endotracheal tube. Normally, intubation took place when someone had quit breathing, and for all her bucking and seizing, the one thing Elena hadn't done yet was quit breathing. But with a belly full of charcoal, the only way to stop her from vomiting it out and sucking it into her lungs was to plug up the pathway, which, in this case, was the trachea. That required a tube in the trachea— a breathing tube. It came with a balloon on the tip of it that could be inflated so nothing at all would pass around the tube, and nothing through it but air or oxygen. Of course, they would have to ventilate her for a while, but that was a small price to pay for saving her life.

"She's still seizing," Caprice said, as she applied the Xylocaine, a local anesthetic that tamped down the gag reflex, to the ET tube.

It was an extraordinarily long seizure, one Adrian had expected to quit by now. But it hadn't, which caused a big problem because as he tried to force her jaw down to insert the tube, she clamped down hard. He couldn't get it in. "I've got to stop the seizure, Caprice," he cried, reaching up to wipe he sweat off his forehead with the back of his arm. "Tube won't go in. Without the tube she'll aspirate, and we don't have a suction machine in here, so we can't keep ahead of it that way." Meaning if they had one, a suction tube could be inserted into Elena's stomach to remove the contents. That would have been the easy way had it been available to them. Unfortunately, it wasn't, which put Elena's life at greater risk. "Can you get that Valium in to her?"

"Done," Caprice said, drawing up a syringe full and injecting it into the IV port. With any luck, that would sedate her enough to get done everything they needed to do.

"Brother Flavian," Adrian called to him, "I need you to come help us. Do you know how to take a blood-pressure reading?"

The monk nodded. "I've helped the doctor here before."

"Can you do that now?"

"Can't," he sputtered, stepping forward, then immediately stepping back.

"Say and prayer and do it," Adrian said, tying not to sound to harsh. The poor man was out of his element here. Scared to death. Feeling guilty over his little mishap. "We need your help and we're both busy."

The man drew in a deep breath, crossed himself, nodded then stepped back to the bed and grabbed the blood-pressure cuff.

"Take it once every minute. We're giving her an elephant's dose of sedative and we need to keep watch."

He nodded as he squeezed the rubber bulb to inflate the cuff.

In the meantime, Adrian attached a tube to the oxygen cylinder Brother Flavian had brought in and readied himself for the next step as Caprice injected the Valium. Elena's seizure had let up for the moment, but she was still rigid, which meant she was still in the throes of it.

"It's not working," Adrian muttered after another minute. Which limited his choices. He could either introduce the tube through her nose and try to get it into her trachea, which wasn't the easiest way of doing things. If he missed, it would go into the esophagus into the stomach, which could trigger more vomiting.

"One ten over seventy-five," Brother Flavian chimed in.

"I found sodium bicarb," Caprice said, as she worked to introduce that into the IV.

"Good," Adrian said. "At least something's going right."

"One hundred over seventy," the monk said.

"Damn," Adrian muttered. "I was afraid that would happen—her blood pressure's dropping rapidly. Sedate her and she crashes."

"Ninety over sixty," from the monk.

"Bicarb's in," Caprice said, putting a stethoscope to her ears to listen to Elena's chest. "It's wet. I think she's probably aspirated some stomach contents."

"Damn," Adrian muttered again, having a try at Elena's jaw to see if the Valium had relaxed her enough yet.

"Eighty-five over fifty-five," said Brother Flavian.

"I've got to go in by nose," Adrian finally said, expecting a protest from Caprice. She knew the risks, especially in a situation such as this. But she merely nodded. "Tube's ready," she said.

At that precise moment Elena bucked so hard she came up off the bed, and when she came back down she went totally limp.

"Can't get her blood pressure," the monk said, frantically pumping up the cuff again.

"In the mouth," Adrian said, taking the laryngoscope from Caprice. "She's not breathing, and we're running out of time. Find me an Ambu-bag." A bag, squeezed manually, used to force breath into the lungs.

With that, he forced Elena's mouth open, glad her jaw had finally relaxed enough to do it, and held her head back enough so that he could visualize the vocal cords. "Perfect," he said, then inserted the breathing tube through the pharynx, past the voice box, and on through to the trachea. It was easy, but what he saw down there made his gut lurch. Elena *had* aspirated charcoal into her lungs already—the blackish color of it was evident in her trachea. He'd thought she probably had, hoped she hadn't. And now he knew. Even though they would get her breathing again, her prognosis wasn't too bright as now she would have to fight aspiration pneumonia, which could well kill her.

He blew up the balloon on the ET tube and taped the tube into place, then checked to make sure Elena's arms were secured tightly to the bed so she wouldn't have an unexpected seizure and rip it out. Adrian wiped the sweat from his brow again and hooked the Ambu-bag up to the tube, taking a good couple of squeezes.

"Eighty-five over fifty-five," Brother Flavian said.

"Going in the right direction, finally," Adrian replied. Now Elena was breathing again. Assisted, of course. But any oxygen into the lungs was good, the bicarb was stabilizing her acidosis, the Valium would keep her quiet. All as good as could be expected. Once the drugs started to wear off, breathing on her own would resume. So, from here on, nothing else would escape into her lungs. Her seizures were over. And, pray God, any pneumonia resulting from the aspirated charcoal would be easily cured once they got her into a proper hospital.

"Pulse is a little stronger," Caprice said, looking over at Adrian, who was standing at the head of the bed, squeezing even breaths into the girl.

Adrian simply nodded, too spent for words. He was thinking about Sean now. Desperately wanting to see him. As a parent, this was the worst thing that could happen…losing a child or coming so close to losing a child…and his heart went out to Mrs Gomez. He couldn't even imagine what she was feeling right now, wasn't going to think about it. In fact, the only thing he wanted to think about when this ordeal was over, and when Sean was back home again, was how he was going to give Sean the biggest hug he'd ever had in his life, even though his son was at the age where hugs and kisses from Dad weren't cool. Didn't matter. Next time he saw Sean, he was going to turn into the most uncool dad there had ever been and hug his son like nobody had ever hugged a child.

"You OK?" he finally managed to ask Caprice, who was busy taking over blood pressure duty from Brother Flavian, who looked on the verge of collapse himself.

"I think that's what I should be asking you, isn't it?" she replied, smiling wearily. "So, are you?"

"Doing fine," he conceded, even though he felt like hell.

"Let me do that," Brother Flavian offered, referring to the ventilating Adrian was doing. "Unless you don't trust me after the botch I've made of things, I can squeeze that bag."

"No botch," Adrian said. "Nobody could have predicted or prevented what happened. And she's doing much better now."

Brother Flavian nodded his head, but the look on his face suggested he wasn't going to forgive himself quite so easily.

"Before you take over, Brother, could you go and call Dr Makela for me and tell him I need him to fly down here right away? Explain what we have going on, tell him to alert the hospital to a critical patient coming in who'll probably need a ventilator," Caprice asked. "Then, if you could, would you send someone over to tell Mrs Gomez that we're taking Elena back to Dulce? Tell her I'll drive and she can ride with me." She paused, then glanced at Adrian. "You'll fly back with Elena, won't you?"

"Are you up to the drive?"

Caprice nodded. "I'll be fine. And I'd feel better having you with Elena in case she has some kind of respiratory episode."

No second guesses or second opinions here. She trusted him, and it felt…good. Made him feel vindicated in some way. Like he was really a part of the team now. "I'll be glad to fly with her." He looked at the monk. "Tell them we'll need a back-up oxygen cylinder and an intubation set-up."

The monk nodded, happy to be any place other than the tiny exam room where Elena had almost died. After he was gone, Caprice moved to the head of the bed and stood next to Adrian. She didn't look at him, though. Rather, she watched his hands squeezing the bag that breathed life into the girl. "You did a good job," she said quietly.

"Remains to be seen," he said flatly, the full force of what had happened finally hitting him.

"At least she's got a chance now. If we hadn't shown up when we did, if you hadn't been able to intubate her the way you did…"

"She aspirated," he snapped.

"Unavoidable risk, and we'll deal with it. Under the circumstances—"

"Circumstances, hell! She aspirated, and that may be an unavoidable risk, but it also an unacceptable one."

"You always so hard on yourself?" Caprice listened to Elena's chest, then pulled her stethoscope from her ears and twined it around her neck. Instinctively, she stepped around behind him and rubbed his shoulders. "Because, from where I was watching, what you pulled off was nothing short of a miracle. You got her intubated and, to be honest, I didn't think that was going to happen. I thought we were going to have to trach her."

Caprice's touch was pure heaven, he thought, sighing the heavy sigh of an emotionally weary man. She had hands like nothing he'd ever felt. Too bad he wasn't in a better mood and in a different situation to enjoy it more.

"What made her do it?" he asked. "She was so far along in her surgeries. And she's old enough to understand the process, so why would she do something like that after all she's been through, and being so close to the end of it all?"

"Age has…has nothing to do with it," she said hesitantly. "There comes a point when you can't be clear-headed about it, I think. You've been ridiculed, you've had surgeries and so many expectations…it's a hard life for someone so young. And if you don't get all the support you need…"

"Your sister?" His voice was gentle, sympathetic.

"My sister," she replied, saying nothing else for a few moments. Finally she continued, "She succeeded in killing herself where Elena failed, and it shocked everybody because we all thought Carlina was braver than that. She always acted brave, always let the hurtful things people said and did roll right off her.

So my family expected her to be brave because she always seemed so strong to us. Of course, maybe that was the easiest way to interpret something we really didn't want to see, or know." Caprice bit off her words, and for the next little while, until Dr Makela arrived to take Elena back to the hospital, she rubbed Adrian's shoulders in silence as he pumped air into Elena, also in silence.

Elena Gomez's stay at Dulce was brief. Just long enough to stabilize her for the trip into San José, to a larger, much better equipped hospital. And now she was no longer their patient. It seemed hollow, without resolution. But realistically she was much better off where she was.

"She's settled in," Adrian told Caprice. "I talked to the doctor on her case and they have her on a ventilator until they can determine the extent of her aspiration pneumonia. But her vital signs are holding steady." Adrian dropped down onto the exam table in Caprice's office and let out a weary sigh. "Blood gases are pretty good and so far there's no sign of internal bleeding from the aspirin." He was tired to the bone. Totally drained. Emotionally and physically exhausted. He'd been the one to fly into San José with Elena, then turn right around and fly back to Dulce once he'd turned over her care. Now he could barely move, barely think.

Never, ever had any flight seemed so long, bagging the girl all that way. By the end of the flight to San José, she had been coming round, though. Not yet conscious, but much lighter in her unconsciousness and breathing a little on her own. Now, for the first time in hours, he was allowing a little optimism over her prognosis to creep in. "I think she's going to make it," he finally said. "Wouldn't have said that a few hours ago, but I'm optimistically cautious. And I think that once Brother Flavian can make arrangements to get Mrs Gomez to San José, she'll see an even bigger change in her daughter."

"I've never thought otherwise," Caprice replied. She was seated at her desk, body slumped down in her chair, shoes off. "You did a good job. I knew you wouldn't let her go."

"Sometimes it's not in our hands," he said. "No matter what we do, other factors come into play…other people's whims and wishes, forces of nature, a higher power, if that's your belief. When I think about all the things that can have an influence in the outcome of someone's recovery, it never seems like I have that much part in it. A pair of hands, a little bit of knowledge and that's about all I can offer."

"I think you underestimate yourself, Adrian. Or downplay your importance or your place."

"Not downplay so much as realize my place." He smiled, thinking of Sean. He'd realized his place in that relationship the instant he'd seen him. Fresh from birth, all red and angry and screaming for everything he was worth, Sean had been *his* from the start, even though at the start he hadn't known Sean wasn't his. He cringed, thinking about that one night of weakness after a very bad day at work when he'd found Sylvie to be the balm he'd needed.

Then she'd disappeared for months, only to return, claiming it was his baby she was about to have. And it had been. Not in the biological sense, but that didn't matter. The first moment he'd set eyes on his son, Adrian had known *his* place in the boy's life. Felt it all the way down to his heart. Other factors coming into play…Sylvie's whims and wishes, forces of nature, a higher power that he *did* believe in…even now, when he thought about all the things that could have had an influence on the outcome of his relationship with his son, he was still amazed. In awe. And grateful it had worked out the way it had. "Tell me about Carlina," he prompted.

"I don't talk about her," she said stiffly, the slump in her tired shoulders now rigid.

"Other than the fact that she committed suicide?"

"Why are you doing this, Adrian? I don't want to talk about her."

"You were the one who did, though. Remember?"

"Bad memories of an ugly time. I didn't mean to say anything."

"There's a lot of story to tell in silence, too, Caprice."

"Why do you want to know?" she cried.

"Because I want to know you. And I have a feeling that what happened to your sister is a big part of you as you blame yourself. You do, don't you?"

"Why do you want to know me?" The defiance in her voice mellowed a bit.

"Believe me, if I weren't so tired right now, I'd come over there and show you. But I can promise you that I'm not budging from this exam table for the next hour or two. So, figure it out for yourself."

"We can't do this, Adrian. I don't—"

"You say you don't get involved, but you drop breadcrumbs along the path. So how do you want me to interpret that, Caprice? Because I think I want to follow those breadcrumbs or at least some of them."

"Physical attraction."

He chuckled. "I'll give you that one, but I don't think you're the type of woman who would ever let a good case of lust govern her life. Not even for a few minutes."

"Who says it's a good case of lust?" she countered.

"It isn't?" He sounded mildly surprised.

"I don't want to talk about it."

Adrian chuckled again. "So, tell me, what do you want to talk about?"

"Nothing. It's time to go fetch Isabella and spend the rest of the evening with her." She stood and headed to the door. "You coming?"

"If I were half the man I was when I got out of bed this morning maybe I would, but right now what's left of me isn't budging."

"Suit yourself." With that, Caprice snapped off the light,

stepped out of the office and shut the door behind her, leaving Adrian alone in the dark, lying flat on the hard, uncomfortable exam table.

In the dark solitude of Caprice's office, he stared up at where he knew the ceiling to be. Somehow he'd imagined that once Elena was stabilized, he and Caprice would meet up like they had, but she would collapse in his arms, tell him the whole story, rather than him collapsing on her exam table and getting nothing. In the better version of this scenario he would comfort her until… Well, he was a man, wasn't he? *Until* was a word weighty with all kinds of possibilities. Except the only possibility that had come to fruition was the hard exam table that would surely give him a kink in the neck by morning. A kink in the neck, and the empty nagging feeling that he truly did want to get to know Caprice in ways he'd promised himself he wouldn't ever with a woman like her.

"Adrian," she whispered, pushing her door open a crack. She'd gone back to her room, spent the rest of the evening playing with Isabella, then when she'd tucked her daughter in for the night, the thought of Adrian sleeping on her exam table got the better of her. The man was a hero and he deserved better than a night on a hard slab. "I have a pillow and a blanket, if you really intend to stay here." Small reward for what he'd done. Ten minutes ago when she'd called the hospital in San José, the nurse in Critical Care had told her that Elena had been awake for a little while, and that she seemed alert. That earned Adrian more than a pillow and a blanket, but a pillow and blanket were the best she could do under the circumstances.

Then there was the way she'd been abrupt with him over Carlina's death. Apologies banked for the future aside, she had, after all, brought up the subject of her sister. Opened the door for him to walk in. Then when he had, by asking more about her, she'd shut him off. Truth was, she never talked to anyone about Carlina—not her life, not her death. Not to her parents. Never to Tony. Especially never to Isabella. It did feel strange that she'd said something to Adrian, but the words had seemed to pop right out. Definitely strange, but in a good way. "Adrian?" she whispered again into the darkness and entered her office.

"Are you returning to tell me you still don't what to talk about it?" he asked, his voice gravelly from sleep.

"I was rude again, wasn't I?" she asked, stepping further in.

"Not rude. Probably understandable."

"It's easier not talking about it. That way, no one gets hurt." Rather than turning on the light, she crept over and laid the blanket down alongside him, then started to turn away. But he grabbed her by the arm and held her there.

"Everyone gets hurt, Caprice. Isabella, because you protect her too much. You, because deep down you don't want to be so alone. You think your armor keeps the pain from getting in, but I think it also keeps it from getting out."

"You don't know…don't understand."

"No, I don't. I've never had someone I love kill themselves, so I can't understand that kind of pain. But I can sympathize with it, if you'd allow me to. Except you won't let anyone do that, will you? It's easier to suffer alone. At least, that's what you think. But I think it's easier when you can share all those emotions, all that pain with someone else who wants to share it with you. That has a way of easing it."

"Easing it?" she hissed, spinning back round to him, catching the outline of his form in the dark. "Do you honestly think there's a way of easing it? I promise you, nothing's going to ease what Elena's mother is feeling tonight."

"Having her daughter alive tonight will ease her pain, Caprice. Maybe not totally wipe it out, but ease it."

"But her guilt?"

"That's the crux of the matter, isn't it?"

"What if it is?"

"How old were you when your sister committed suicide?" he asked, his voice as gentle as the dark surrounding them. "And you took on all that blame?"

"We've gone through this before and I still want to know what difference could any of it possibly make to you?"

"You know, I've been lying here asking myself the same thing for quite a while now, and I don't have an answer for you. Maybe I simply want to be your friend. Or maybe I want more. Hard to know which one it is as I've barely had a go at the one, and the other is a delusion which even I recognize. And if you knew the crazy mess my life is in it would confound you even more than the way you hide yourself confounds me. But that's it. And as for why I care? I'm open to theories, here. Meaning if I'm smart, I should probably go on the assumption that I'm pitching a feeble attempt at friendship, and leave it at that. OK?" He let go of her arm, then sat up. "Think it's time to head back to my room now that I've got my second wind, get a good night's sleep…" His words were casual with a little bit of a chilly nip to them as he swung his legs over the side of the exam table. "And try not to remember that any of this conversation ever happened." Once he was fully upright, Adrian stopped short of standing when Caprice stepped in front of him.

"More?" she asked. "When you said it might be something more, could you define that?"

"That's not what you want," he said, his voice suddenly low. "Trust me, Caprice, we can't do this."

"And I don't have a choice?"

Adrian chuckled. "If I thought for a moment this was really your choice…" He stopped, cleared his throat, then continued. "I can do a sexual fling, if that's what you want. And, believe me, it's been on my mind more than once since I met you. It would be easy to do, too. Right here, right now." He patted the spot on the exam table next to him. "Lock the door, leave the lights off…or on, if that's what you like. Then we both get an itch scratched. But what about tomorrow, when you wake up and the smile is gone from your face and you have to work with me at the head of your surgical table? If I thought you were the kind of woman who could merely sleep with a man then brush it off like it's nothing, I'd already be naked. But you're not. Everything affects you too deeply, which is probably one of the reasons why I'm attracted to you. And confused by you."

Adrian raised his hand to brush her cheek, and Caprice caught it in her hand and kissed his palm. "Wouldn't you know that the one and only time in my life I decide to do something a little crazy, I'm with a gentleman."

"With you, Caprice, I wouldn't be a gentleman."

"With me, Adrian, I wouldn't want you to be. It would be disappointing." She stepped closer to him, nudging her way in between his legs, then raised her arms and twined her fingers around his neck. "You're right, though. We can't do this."

"Another step closer, and it will already be done."

Pulling his face close to hers, she laughed. "It can be done without another step." Inching her face to Adrian's, she kissed him almost shyly, surprised by the taste of him on her lips. Sweet, and a little salty. Had it been so long that she'd forgotten? Or had Tony never tasted this good? And this was good. Soft lips, parting as her tongue ventured to probe inside. He didn't kiss back, but didn't resist. More like he relaxed into her exploration…tongue to tongue, tongue sliding over that sensitive spot just inside the lip, tongue delving deeper… Nice. She wanted more. She wanted his response.

She pushed herself hard against Adrian's body. He shifted on top of the exam table, moving himself closer to the edge of it, closer to her, until he was partially standing and she was so tight against him she could feel his erection pressing against her pelvis. For a man who'd said he didn't want this...

Suddenly Adrian's arms were around her and he was returning her kiss. Hard and swift. Raw and full of need.

Shivers of desire streaked through her body, and for the first time in her life she knew what it felt like to succumb to someone else. She was succumbing to Adrian. She wanted to, and tomorrow be damned. This was about tonight. Right now. This very moment.

As his tongue probed her mouth, it was more forceful than hers had been. The exploration not shy at all. He took. Nibbled. Teased. Until her knees were weak. Then he grabbed her by the bottom, rocking his pelvis against her, and the hardness of his erection crushed her, heightening her need, as their bodies found a rhythm.

Caprice closed her eyes to savor the total feel of this, to picture, in her mind, every little nuance of what she couldn't see in the dark, and when she did, his hand slipped underneath her T-shirt to discover that she'd removed her bra earlier. Instinctively, he went for her breast...her nipple...and it was already pebble-hard in anticipation as he pinched it between his thumb and index finger. An involuntary gasp escaped her, one that, unfortunately, broke the moment, for Adrian pulled his hand out from under her shirt and in the same swift motion gave her a gentle shove away from him.

"We don't want this," he said, his voice heavy, almost harsh.

"Says who?" Caprice asked, her own voice heavy, too.

Adrian scooted himself carefully back on the exam table, taking care to break all physical contact with Caprice. "We did. Over and over. To each other. You probably to yourself. Me to myself. Common sense dictating."

Caprice cleared her throat as she pulled her shirt back into place. "Too bad we both have so much common sense," she muttered, somewhat glad and somewhat sad for the way this had turned out. "Way too much common sense." With that, she turned and headed to the door, her knees still weak, her nipples still hard. Once there, she turned back, saw only the silhouette of Adrian in the dark, and sighed. "And damn you, Adrian, for being such a gentleman," she said with absolutely no animosity in her voice whatsoever.

"Damn me, too," he muttered, as the door clicked closed.

CHAPTER SEVEN

"WHERE is she?" Caprice asked Josefina.

It was barely daylight, but Caprice had already been at work for two hours. First, she'd called about Elena, who was already extubated and off the ventilator and doing very nicely physically, although she refused to speak to anyone, including her mother, who was at her side now.

Relieved by the news, Caprice had dropped in to spend a few minutes with each of her surgical patients, all short procedures for today—a third and probably final surgery for Raphael Montez, a patient with a mildly cleft lip scheduled for scar reduction, a fifth and not nearly the last surgery for Jorge Villa, a little boy scheduled for a cleft lip rhinoplasty that would correct the asymmetry of his nose and help his breathing, and then Consuela Hernandez, who needed a septoplasty to correct her deviated septum and also alleviate a breathing problem.

Milestones for these children as they began or ended their journey, and Caprice always took time before surgery to simply sit with them, and their parents, to answer questions, allay fears, hold hands. Going into surgery was a frightening thing for both child and parent, she knew from experience, and the little kindnesses mattered so much.

So this morning she'd gone through her round of last-minute

explanations, done a few preliminary quick checks on her patients, and now, one hour until the official start to her surgical day and she was desperate for a few minutes alone with Isabella. Perhaps breakfast in the garden, or a short walk at the jungle's edge.

But Isabella wasn't in the room when Caprice got there. Instead, she found Josefina, who was sitting by the window, sipping a cup of coffee and reading a book.

"Dr Adrian took her," Josefina explained. "They went to have breakfast together."

"You just let him take her?" she asked, annoyed and disappointed. "Without asking me?"

"I don't normally ask you when you're working." Josefina shrugged, totally unconcerned. "You've never required that I do. So when Dr Adrian stopped by and Isabella was happy to see him, I let her go with him. You didn't tell me you would come back this morning, so I thought it would be good for her to spend some time with him…they always get along well."

"They've done this before?" She didn't know if she was angry or hurt that she hadn't been included in this part of Isabella's life. Not to know what was going on with Isabella… A dull queasiness settled in her stomach as she thought about it. Her little girl was growing up, getting a life of her own, a life where she wasn't the center of it. It was an odd feeling, realizing so much time was ticking off the clock. Odd, sad, frightening.

Josefina nodded. "Yes, they've done this a few times, but only for a little while. And she always seems so happy when she comes back."

Now she was stunned. Not because this was happening, but because nobody had even had the decency to tell her. Not her daughter, not even the man she'd thrown herself at last night. More evidence of how quickly Isabella was growing up—when she herself was watching and when she wasn't. Another wave of queasiness rolled through her, but it didn't have quite the same impact as the heaviness settling into her heart. Somehow, in all these years with Isabella, she'd never seen this coming. Call her oblivious, call her in denial, call her anything you wanted, but she'd simply never considered the day when her daughter wouldn't need her so much. And that hurt.

More than the pain, though, she felt something else. Anger, disappointment, and…was it jealousy? Was she *jealous* that Isabella was so drawn to Adrian? No, that was silly. She was just…well, she wanted to claim surprise, but she'd seen them that day when he'd arrived and Isabella had taken to him immediately. So she'd known the effect he could have on her daughter, which made her…oblivious, didn't it? Or maybe she had a complete blind spot when it came to Isabella. Had she turned into one of those parents who couldn't separate their wishes for their child from their child's wishes for themselves? Whatever it was, it was time to do some deep introspection on her relationship with Isabella, sort out where they were now and how they were still going to change, as time couldn't be turned back, much as she wished it could. Isabella was growing up and becoming the independent person Caprice had always hoped she would be. Of course, Caprice hadn't counted on that independence hurting so fiercely. "Next time, ask my permission *first* before you allow her to go off with *anybody*," she said, spinning away from Josefina and heading into the hall, knowing full well that had been a reactionary response to something that hadn't merited reaction.

"Does that include her children friends?" Josefina called after her, her voice razor-sharp. "And do you need to approve her friends now? Line them up, pick them out, give them your stamp of approval?"

Caprice stopped, then turned back. Josefina's words had been pointed and they'd pierced her straight between the shoulders. She was right, of course. Caprice knew that. She also knew that Adrian had said much the same thing to her a while ago, that she was being too protective. But she couldn't change in the blink of an eye, not after spending so many years being protective. "Is it too much to ask to be allowed in on decisions concerning my daughter's activities and friends?" she asked, but not in an accusatory manner, as at heart she knew what she had to do, even though she was being stubborn about doing it.

"Is it too much to allow Isabella to make some decisions for herself?" Josefina countered. "She's growing up, has a mind of her own." The sharp scowl on her face melted into a kindly smile. "She's like you in so many ways, if you haven't noticed. Very smart, very independent. And at such a young age. You should be proud she's doing so well."

"I am," Caprice whispered. "And I'm scared, too. There are so many things that can still hurt her."

"Not Dr Adrian. He's good with Isabella, and he tries to be her friend, not her…protector. You're a good mother, Caprice. But you've got to let Isabella go just a little when she needs it. Right now, she needs it." She smiled sympathetically. "We all have to do it…let our children grow, and eventually go. But they come back to us. I promise you, they do."

This was why she trusted Josefina as she trusted no one else with Isabella. "But it's not easy. I think you'll have to keep reminding me for a while." Caprice glanced at her watch. "Look, I'll be breaking from surgery around one for lunch, if everything goes well. Do you think I could have lunch with her?"

Josefina smiled. "I think she would like for you to ask her sometimes, instead of telling her. Respect her choice. Like I said, she's like you, and you don't take it so well when somebody tells you, instead of asking."

Caprice laughed. Yes, Josefina was truly a godsend and she adored the woman for her honesty and for the way she loved Isabella. "I'm glad you're not subtle with me. Subtlety doesn't always work because sometimes I'm awfully…"

"Hard-headed," Josefina supplied, assuming the position to continue reading her book.

"That fits," Caprice admitted. "So, do you know where they went?"

"To the gardens. If you hurry, they might invite you to breakfast with them."

"Or, if I don't hurry, maybe Isabella will start to realize that I respect her independence."

Yes, it was difficult watching her little girl grow up and she wasn't doing a good job of it. But she was growing up, too, in a lot of ways, and allowing Isabella this time with Adrian was part of the process for Isabella, as well as for her.

Suddenly Caprice was slapped with a new feeling…one she'd never had before. It was a quiver of fear, maybe uncertainty for the day Isabella found her own life—her own totally independent life. It was still years away, but years had a way of going too quickly. When that happened, when Isabella was out on her own, *and that would eventually happen,* what then?

Like she needed more emotional turmoil, a deep-down feeling of aloneness settled in, one Caprice knew wouldn't be shaken off easily, and one that would keep coming back to stab her, probably for years to come, each and every time Isabella moved away from her in even the least little fashion.

There was going to come a day when the inevitable void in her life would take hold, then what? Her mind went to Adrian for a moment, to possibilities she'd come so close to exploring, then she blocked out that thought. A near one-night stand, or even one that might happen, didn't equate to a future. More like it was an isolated moment in time, just like Adrian. In a few days his obligation here would end and he'd return to Miami. Eventually she would return to California and maybe, occasionally, their paths would cross. But that was nothing. Absolutely nothing. Which was what she wanted, of course.

Yet, the thought of nothing with Adrian…

"But do you respect it?" Josefina asked. "Do you truly respect her independence, or are you saying that only to sound good to your own ears?"

"I suppose that's something I'll have to figure out, isn't it?" she replied despondently. Truth was, she didn't know. Didn't know about Isabella, didn't know about Adrian. At the moment, didn't know much about anything.

"No," Isabella said in all seriousness. "That's *not* a gorilla. There are no gorillas in Costa Rica. It's a sp-spider monkey."

Adrian and Isabella were sitting on a bench on the lawn at the jungle's edge, watching a little spider monkey jumping from branch to branch in the trees and bushes. It was watching them as intently as they were watching it, or rather it was watching their breakfast fruit feast of anonas and guavas and paw-paws, or perhaps it was more interested in the fresh tortillas made just a while ago in the hospital kitchen. Whatever the case, there was a wary watchfulness going on, and Adrian was glad to be sharing it with Isabella. It eased a little of his longing for Sean. "Have you ever seen a gorilla?" he teased.

"No, but I've seen a spider monkey before. And my mother told me what a gorilla is."

"Has she ever seen a gorilla?" he asked, fighting back the urge to laugh.

Isabella paused for a moment, a tiny frown creasing her brow. "I'll have to as-ask her."

"You do that," he said, handing her half an anona, a strange-looking, heart-shaped fruit with sweet, milk-white pulp. It was eaten with a spoon, the outer brownish-red skin serving as a bowl. "Then get back to me on it, because I've never seen a gorilla myself. Not in person, anyway."

"Or a sp-spider monkey," Isabella teased.

"How'd you get so smart?" he asked, handing her a spoon and a napkin.

Isabella nodded her head seriously. "From my m-mother. She's smart, too. It's called heredity. Sometimes it's good, sometimes it's bad, depending on what you get from it."

She sounded so much like Caprice. He really liked this child. So serious and so young, and still so innocent. What a perfect delight! "And getting smart from heredity is good," he stated, watching the spider monkey make its way down the palm tree.

"It's better than getting d-dumb from it." Isabella giggled.

"You *are* your mother's daughter, aren't you?" he said, laughing. Amazing little girl. In spite of being over-protective, Caprice was doing a brilliant job of raising her. Single parenting wasn't easy. He knew that all too well. But success always showed in the child, and Caprice was such a success at this. Probably more than he'd initially given her credit for.

Adrian made a mental note to pay her the compliment next time he saw her. Then he pushed aside the mental image that had played in his mind over and over since last night. It was for the best. He'd said that a thousand times since then, and if he kept saying it to himself, maybe in another thousand times he'd actually believe it.

"Huh?" Isabella gave him a curious look, clearly not understanding his comment.

"It means your heredity has served you well."

"Do you have any children?" she asked, out of the blue.

"One," he said. "His name is Sean. He's a little younger than you."

"S-Sean. Did his heredity serve him well?" she asked, fighting herself to say the words perfectly.

Tough question to answer. From Sean's mother there was nothing, and God only knew who his biological father was. "He's done well in spite of it," Adrian answered. Truth was, even with

Sylvie's interference Sean was a well-adjusted little boy in every sense of the definition. "He's done very well, I think." And pray that continued after this round with Sylvie.

"Do you miss him?"

"Like crazy." More than he could put into words.

"Where is he now?"

"With his…his mother."

"Your wife?"

"Not for a very long time."

"Divorced, like my mother?" Isabella asked. "She hasn't been married for a very long time, you know. But I th-think it's time. Is it time for you to get married again?"

The child was matchmaking! And none too subtly. Cute. Misplaced, but cute. "I think it's time to give this spider monkey a piece of paw-paw," he said, glad for the distraction as the monkey crept closer. Cute little distraction, he thought, glad it had captured Isabella's attention with its begging. About the length of a newborn baby, with red and brown fur, its tail exceeded the length of its body by a third and its long, curved paws twitched in anticipation as it neared them cautiously. Somewhere deep in the jungle directly in front of them Adrian heard a call like the whinnying of a horse. Probably a mate eager to have a piece of the paw-paw and telling this one to hurry up, he decided, holding out a piece to tempt the monkey.

As it made its way slowly across the grass, its tail pulled up parallel to its back, Isabella grabbed hold of Adrian's arm in eager anticipation. "Can I do it?" she whispered. "Can I f-feed him?"

The protective father in Adrian took over and he shook his head. "He might bite," Adrian whispered back.

"Won't he bite you, then?" she inquired in all innocence.

The child bordered on being too bright, he thought as the monkey crept close enough for Adrian to toss the piece of fruit to it. As he raised his hand, though, Isabella shifted positions, causing him to jerk the paw-paw and scare the monkey, which in turn made the monkey lunge for the fruit and, in doing so, nip Adrian's finger.

Isabella squealed in excitement, not noticing Adrian's injury, the monkey screeched in fear and ran away with its piece of paw-paw, and Adrian sat there looking down at the drop of blood on his fingertip, with the issue of rabies springing to mind immediately.

"Can we do that again?" Isabella asked, grabbing another piece of paw-paw to coax the monkey back.

"I think he's probably had enough for today," Adrian replied, grabbing a paper napkin to wrap around his finger. And even if the monkey hadn't had enough, he had. Especially when he turned around and saw Caprice standing in the gardens, watching and laughing.

"He barely broke the skin," she said, holding Adrian's hand under the running stream of water from the sink in her exam room. She'd watched them for a while, watched the interaction between them. She'd been tempted to move closer to listen to their conversation, but had resisted. The one thing she hadn't been able to resist, though, had been watching, and what she'd seen between Adrian and Isabella had been nice. Comfortable. Trusting. Too bad her daughter couldn't have a relationship like that with her father, but that would never happen.

Of course, the spider monkey had rather interrupted a good thing. "I'll give you an antibiotic and you'll be fine."

"Rabies," Adrian muttered, definitely grumpy.

"From bats, usually. You weren't trying to feed any bats this morning, were you?" she teased.

"Funny," he snorted.

Caprice patted Adrian's hand dry with a towel, applied a dab of ointment to his finger, then wrapped it in a small bandage. "Good as new," she said, stepping back to appraise her handiwork. "Oh, and thank you for not letting Isabella feed the monkey. She would, you know. Just stick her hand right out there with a piece of fruit, not thinking about the consequences…" She stopped, feigning a look of innocence. "Oh, that's right. You did that, didn't you?"

"Very funny," he quipped, jamming the wounded hand into his pocket.

"You should have let go before he jumped at you."

"Now you tell me."

She smiled. "You and Isabella get along quite well."

"You've done a good job with her. She was explaining how the good parts of her are a matter of good heredity, and that—"

"We have surgery," Caprice snapped, spinning around abruptly. "I don't have time to stand around and talk."

Adrian blinked his surprise at her change in attitude, then stepped in front of the door, refusing to let her leave. "What's going on, Caprice? One minute we're having a nice talk about your daughter, and the next you've turned into a glacier. Your banked apologies are used up, and now I'd like an explanation."

"It's none of your business."

"If it's something I said, then it is," he said, his voice gentle. Adrian reached out to stroke her cheek, but she slapped his hand away.

"One kiss doesn't give you the right to anything, Adrian."

"As I recall, you wanted more than a kiss."

"My mistake," she snapped.

"It wasn't a mistake, Caprice. Maybe pushing you away was, but you being there last night, wanting it, wasn't. And that, if nothing else, entitles me to a little something from you. Just an explanation. That's all I'm asking for. One minute you're fine, but then the next… I don't even know how to explain it."

Caprice pulled away from him, then turned her back. He was right. She did owe him something. No matter what her intentions had been when Adrian had arrived in Costa Rica, he'd twisted his way in, made himself a part of her life in a way she wasn't yet ready to explore. But to tell him this…the thing she'd never told anyone?

She drew in a deep breath. Yes, perhaps it was time. And perhaps when she told him all the ugly details he'd see her for what she was and leave her alone. That would be for the best. For everyone.

Caprice turned back around to Adrian. "Isabella's cleft palate was my fault. A matter of heredity that wasn't so good for her." She drew in a deep breath, bracing herself to say the next words. "My sister, Carlina, the one who committed suicide…she…" The words wouldn't come.

"She had a cleft palate?" he asked softly.

Caprice nodded. "Not corrected when she was young. My parents couldn't afford it, my father's insurance wouldn't cover it. So Carlina suffered so much ridicule for a long time before anything was done to help her."

"Which is why you knew so much about Elena's struggles and feelings. You lived through them with your sister."

She looked up at Adrian through a teary blur. "That's the thing. I didn't live through it with her. I was young, embarrassed. I saw my own father's aversion to her. So I stayed away. Let my friends make fun. Laughed when other people did. And all she ever wanted was to be accepted…even a little acceptance from the people she loved. She got it from my mother, but never from my father and never from me. Then when she killed herself…"

Caprice's voice broke, and Adrian pulled her into his arms. "You were just a child," he said, holding her close, letting her sob into his chest. "Children do mean things. You yourself say that all the time."

"But she was my sister," she said, her voice muffled by the fabric of his shirt. "It shouldn't have mattered to me. I should have been her sister, her friend. I should have defended her, but I—"

"The acts of a child, sweetheart. That's all it was."

"Except she killed herself, and I never told her…she never knew…"

"I'm sorry," he whispered into her hair. "I wasn't there, and I don't know for sure, but I can't see you ever being as cruel as you think you were. You're still seeing it as a child, reacting as the child would. But you wouldn't have always been like that to your sister. You don't have it in you."

She looked up at him, the tears streaking down her cheeks. "We all have it in us, Adrian. Which is why I chose this as my life's work. To make it up to Carlina. It's not enough, can never be enough, but it's all I can do."

He brushed away her tears with his thumb then pulled her head back to her chest. "It's a worthy reason for a worthy cause, but you don't deserve the guilt you're carrying. Even if there were times you weren't nice to your sister, you don't deserve a lifetime of misery over it. We all make mistakes. It's what we do about those mistakes that counts, and what you've done is amazing. Carlina would be proud of you, sweetheart. You've turned her struggles into the smiling faces of so many children like her, and that does count for something."

"But then I had Isabella, with her cleft palate," she said. "A hereditary condition, the doctor told me after she was born."

"And I'll bet your first reaction to her wasn't aversion or embarrassment, was it?"

She shook her head. "All I could think of was how Carlina had struggled and how I didn't want Isabella to struggle the same way." She pushed herself away from Adrian, then walked over to her desk to grab a tissue. After she'd blown her nose, she turned back to face him. "Tony took one look at Isabella and, instead of being happy about her, the first thing he said, in front of the doctors and nurses, was that I had to have a hysterectomy before he'd ever have sex with me again. He said he didn't want to risk bringing another monster into the world, and that, apparently, I was a carrier."

"Bastard," Adrian hissed.

"Maybe, but he was honest. And he was also expressing the same thing I saw in my own father's face when Carlina went to him for affection or attention. My father wasn't so cruel outwardly, like Tony, but he was repulsed by his daughter, the way my husband was repulsed by his. The moment Isabella was born, I swore—"

"To protect her at all costs," he supplied. "To the exclusion of having anything in your life other than your work and your daughter."

"It worked out," she said, her voice going stiff. "My husband never came near me again. Not once. I thought, for a while, that after he saw how the surgeries could improve Isabella's condition he'd get over it and we'd be the family we'd talked about being when I was pregnant with her. I was deluding myself, of course. And the more I hung onto my marriage, kidding myself that it would get better, the more I resented him for the way he felt about Isabella…his flesh and blood."

"So now you push everybody else away."

"Because it's easier."

"For who?" he asked. "Isabella, or you? Because I had breakfast with an amazing little girl who thinks it's time for her mother to marry again."

"She craves a daddy."

"She's entitled to," Adrian responded. "But don't you crave something else in your life, too?"

Caprice drew in a ragged breath. "When you asked who it was easier for…the answer is me. It's easier for me to push everybody away."

"Like you pushed your sister away?" he asked. "You think you don't deserve someone to love you because you pushed your sister away?"

"I didn't have the hysterectomy, Adrian. As a doctor, you know the physical reasons why I couldn't do that, but I did have a tubal ligation. I was actually trying to save my marriage. And I've regretted it ever since."

"Sometimes they can be reversed."

"Why? What would be the point?"

"Maybe to get over your husband once and for all. Maybe so, in the end, he won't have had the last word over your life. Not all men would look at a child like Isabella and call her a monster, you know. There are some who would love her the way her mother does."

"But there are so many who wouldn't, and that's all I have in my life. My own father has never seen Isabella. Said he never would. So, tell me, how can I trust something I've never had in my life?" She grabbed one more tissue from the box, wiped the tears from her face, blew her nose again, then straightened her shoulders. "We have a patient being prepped for surgery now. I'll see you there in ten minutes."

With that, Caprice whipped past Adrien, pulled open the door with an angry tug, then marched straight into the hall. Ten paces away from her exam room, though, the starch left her shoulders and she veered into the nearest ladies' room for one more good cry.

"She said what?" Adrian snapped, strangling the receiver of the payphone he was holding it so tight. He glanced at the clock on the wall. Five minutes late for surgery already, and Caprice was probably going to be good and angry about it. Especially as she'd opened up to him the way she'd done. But he couldn't help it. After breakfast with Isabella, then after everything Caprice had told him, he simply needed to hear if there was any word on Sean. Which there was. Sylvie had finally made contact.

Ben exhaled an obviously pained sigh. "She said she wants a lump settlement this time, that she doesn't want child support coming in installments any more. And that if you can't agree to her terms, she's going to court to petition for full custody of Sean, that maybe his real father will come up with some money."

"His real father?" Adrian choked. "Did she say who that was?"

All these years, Sylvie had claimed not to know. Not that it mattered to Adrian. But if she did know, and if Sean's real father wanted him… A sick lump formed in his gut. This was getting worse just when he'd thought it couldn't.

"Not a word. As far as I know, this is the first time there's ever been a mention of his real father. I think it's probably a threat because if she knew who that was, we'd have seen some interaction there a long time ago. She'd have brought him into the equation much earlier than this. So I'm not going to worry about that."

"I'm not either because I'm his real father, damn it! His *only* parent. Nobody else has the right to say that. Not his biological father if he comes forward, not Sylvie…"

"We'll get it all worked out in court," Ben assured him.

Worked out…how? Would he be fighting two parents for Sean now, instead of one? Would a biological father who might not have known his son existed want his son when he found out he had one?

Suddenly the hall walls were closing in around him, his life was closing in and there was nowhere to go. The grip of angry frustration tight around his throat, Adrian grabbed the phone book chained to the payphone, ripped the chain from its anchor to the phone's wall mount, and threw it at the opposite wall. "Did you talk to Sean?" he asked, fighting to regain control before he did something more drastic.

"No. Sylvie said he was busy playing and she didn't want to interrupt him, but that he was fine. I did ask if you could speak to him."

"And?" He held his breath for the answer.

"She said no. But I told her that you're angry right now, and not inclined to co-operate with her. That maybe, if you could talk to Sean for a few minutes, the anger would give way to missing him, or desperation, or some kind of emotion that would make you give in to her."

Good twist, Adrian thought. But would it work on Sylvie? She wasn't stupid after all. "What did she say?"

"She'd think about it," Ben said. "And get back to me when she's decided. It's the best I could do, Adrian. The lady wants money, and now, with the threat of bringing a biological father into this, I don't want to push her. And I sure as hell don't want her to think we're going after her legally this time. So I told her that would be acceptable, and to let me know what she decides, one way or the other."

"I want him back, Ben. Whatever it takes. Whatever you have to do to make it right." He glanced at the clock again, and imagined Caprice pacing the floor of the surgical suite, muttering some very unkind and probably very explicit things about him. "I want it over so we can get back to our normal life." Only right now he wasn't even sure if he remembered what normal was. Briefly, he wondered if there was a place in his and Sean's normalcy for Caprice and Isabella. Then he wiped that thought from his mind and replaced it with the image of his son. One thing at a time. He had a life to solve, and he sure as hell didn't need someone else in his life who couldn't solve her own life. Didn't need that at all. "Let me know the minute you hear," he said, then hung up and ran to the surgical wing, expecting the very worst from Caprice.

After the ten minutes it took him to scrub up, get into his gown, tie on his mask and snap on his gloves, then enter the surgical theater, it was a surprise that Caprice was the only one who wasn't there.

CHAPTER EIGHT

"YOU OK?" Adrian asked, pulling off his surgical mask and throwing it into the trash. "I was concerned when you were late." The surgery had gone well. She'd whisked in five minutes after he had scrubbed, performed a perfect operation, no explanation offered for her tardiness. And throughout the entire procedure she'd barely even glanced at him. He'd noticed that. Thought it was odd. Of course, he could be reading something into nothing. But her manner had been...well, if he had to put a word to the way she'd acted, it was brusque.

In fact, she was still being brusque, staring at him over her surgical mask now, even though the surgery was over, and the patient was already resting in Recovery. "I'm OK," she said, her voice as flat as he'd ever heard it. "Just fine."

"You're sure? Because you're not acting fine."

"I'm not acting fine because I've been giving this thing going on between us a lot of thought, and I want you to leave me alone, Adrian. We're coming too close. On the verge of something I *don't* want." She was trying hard to sound as hard as stone but her voice was beginning to give way, getting a littler higher than its normal low, throaty pitch, sounding on the verge of a tremble. "I was in an emotional state before surgery *because of you*, and I can't operate that way. I'm not blaming you, but you did get me talking about things I have never talked about, experiencing emotions I'd put away years ago, and even though that wasn't your intent, it was the result. I just can't go through that again. It takes too much out of me, which could endanger my patients. So, whatever this is that's going on between us, Adrian, it's got to stop. I can't deal with it. I'm not here to get involved with you, or anyone else, and even though I've made that perfectly clear, I've been the one to slip up. So I've got to back off. You do, too, and it's my fault as much as it is yours. Probably more."

She pulled off her disposable surgical cap and threw it impatiently into the trash. "I'm not blaming you for any of this, but I am asking you to please leave me alone and respect my wishes in this."

"But you would have slept with me," he said, making sure to keep his voice low, even though there was no one else in the surgical scrub room to overhear them. "You were the one who came to me, and the one who suggested that we might…"

Agitated, Caprice jerked out her hand, palm facing him, to stop him, then she withdrew it and with an exasperated huff of breath ran it through her hair. "I know I did. I'm admitting it. I had a moment of weakness, and what I'm also admitting is that I'd probably do it again if the right situation arose between us. I haven't been with a man in years, Adrian. *Not in years!* Haven't even been tempted until now. And you tempt me. Tempt me like crazy, and I'm not even ashamed or embarrassed to admit it. It gets lonely. *I get lonely.* That, combined with the attraction I've had for you, became a problem. A big problem that I can't deal with. I'm so attracted to you that I've got to make myself push you away."

Caprice paused for a moment, walked over to the hamper, pulled off the soiled surgical gown that covered her scrubs and tossed it in. Then she turned back to Adrian. "Right now, though, I'm going through some emotional things…facing the fact that Isabella's growing up and starting into a life of her own that doesn't include me at the center, facing newly emerging feelings about my sister that I thought were buried deep. Mixed emotions, conflicts, low points, they're all getting to me. And what scares me most is that I let down my resolve and the first thing I wanted when I did was you. I mean, I'm not one of those idiots who denies those kinds of feelings or tries giggling them away. Truth is, I could go to bed with you right here and now if I let myself. Except I can't let it happen, and I need you to help me get through this."

I'm so attracted to you that I've got to make myself push you away. Was she kidding? Did she expect him to heap praise on her for her deep insight and restraint? Then expect him to step in a take over when her resolve failed? What about his own feelings here? Had she ever once considered that pushing her away from him might be just as difficult as her pushing herself away from him? "Let me get this straight," he began, forcing himself to sound controlled about this, when what he really wanted to do was explode at her. "You're asking me to help *you* not sleep with *me*? You get to be weak about this because I have to be strong? Is that what you want? Because I resisted you once, Caprice, and it was a damn hard thing to do. How the hell can you expect me to resist you again if you offer it, when I was barely able to resist you the first time? And, baby, you have no idea how hard that was for me."

Angry, frustrated and going through a whole lot of other emotions he wasn't even sure he could label, Adrian spun around to the sink to begin scrubbing for their second surgery. Tapping on the faucet's foot pedal to start the water flowing, he stuck his arms under the warm spray and let it trickle down to his fingertips before he punched the soap dispenser. But before the soap drizzled out he spun back around to Caprice, his arms dripping wet, his face set in controlled anger.

"You know, I really have a problem with women who have issues. My life has gone to hell and back because of them, and I promised myself a long time ago that if I *ever* got involved in a serious relationship again, she wouldn't have parental issues, divorce issues, professional issues of any kind. And you, Caprice, are a walking suitcase full of them. I like you. I think you're a fantastic mother, even if too over-protective of Isabella. I admire your skills as a surgeon and you have wonderful compassion toward your patients that I've rarely ever seen in any other surgeon. All good qualities, and on top of that you're gorgeous. If I could take you to bed and leave your issues behind, I would do it in a heartbeat because I'm totally attracted to you, and I'm not exactly a saint in that department. But I can't do that because all those issues are a big part of you. You can't get away from them, and I'm not saying that to be mean or to hurt you. I'm merely being observant. Telling it the way I see it. So, I think that in the interests of what's best for both of us, let's keep this professional between us—no small talk, no personal talk, nothing that isn't about the job here and now—because you obviously don't need me in your life in any capacity other than anesthesiologist, and I sure don't want you as anything but the doctor performing the surgery at my table. So I suppose that pretty well defines us, doesn't it?"

Caprice stepped back, stunned, feeling like she'd just been slapped. First it had been Josefina being so blunt with her about Isabella, and now Adrian. She supposed she deserved it, as she wasn't so vain as to admit that she didn't own the fault for their reactions. Still, it was brutal. Not easy to hear. Even more difficult to admit that they were both right about this. While she still had a smidgen of pride left, though, she was going to do the best thing for everyone concerned. Including her patients.

"Yes, I suppose it does define us," she replied. "And I think it best that, starting this afternoon, you'll be assigned to work with Dr Snowden in his operating theater. He's an excellent surgeon, and very cordial. Doesn't let all those sticky personal issues get in the way of his working relationships. I'll let him know to expect you with the afternoon rounds, and you can prep through lunchtime with his patient charts to get acquainted with what you'll be doing."

"I didn't want to change things medically between us, Caprice," Adrian said without inflection. "Just personally."

"Neither did I, but I'm afraid all this honestly is going to make it quite uncomfortable between us from now on, on any level." If not for him, then for her. She'd been the one stepping over her own imposed line, and he knew it. He was truly a gentleman not to bring that up, but that didn't change the matter. It wasn't an easy thing to face, and she feared that every time she looked up at him during a procedure, remembering that she'd been the one to make the first move would pop into her mind. She simply couldn't have that. Wouldn't have that. Not at the expense of any of her patients. "I think we can probably get on professionally for the rest of your time here, but besides all the *issues* I have, we now have a little issue of our own, don't we? And there's no place for that at the operating table. So we separate and the only person who really counts in this—the patient—wins."

Caprice tried to force a polite smile as she finally pulled down her surgical mask, but she wasn't sure that what was registering on her face was a polite smile or more a grimace of agony. For at the moment agony was what she felt. Total, complete agony. And, surprisingly, that sense of aloneness again. "I'm sorry, Adrian," she whispered, tossing her mask into the trash. "It should have worked out better between us, and I'm sorry that it didn't."

"I'm sorry, too," Adrian replied, turning back to the sinks then dipping his arms under the water for a scrub. "I would have liked to work with you more in the surgical theater…and slept with you afterwards. We would have been good together, both places."

She glanced over at him, smiling wistfully. "Be careful what you wish for, Doctor. Sometimes you do get it." Then when you did, sometimes you didn't want it. Just like she didn't want to go back to being professional only with Adrian. But she'd gotten her wish about that, and now she had to live with it. Be careful what you wish for, indeed!

Isabella led her mother to the spot where she'd seen the spider monkey earlier. "It was right up there in the tr-tree," she said. "Watching me and Adrian."

"Adrian and me," Caprice corrected.

Isabella nodded. "He didn't know about spider monkeys, so I had to tell him."

"You did?" Caprice asked, laughing. "That was awfully nice of you." This was what made everything worthwhile, these times with her daughter. Even if she had only a few moments over a brief lunch, she always felt refreshed afterwards, always felt like those *issues* to which Adrian had referred no longer existed. "So, what else did you and Adrian talk about?" she asked, not so much to be nosey but to keep the conversation going as Isabella was already distracted, looking for another monkey.

"His divorce," she answered, quite carefree about it all.

Caprice blinked over that one. "Adrian's divorce? He talked about his divorce with you?" Odd topic to be discussing with a child. Very odd!

"No, I t-talked about it with him. And about your divorce."

Her grown-up daughter was talking about divorce? About her divorce from Tony! It was a part of Isabella's life for sure, so she wasn't surprised it was of interest to her. Still, it was a shock to hear her discussing it with such a lack of concern. More than that, though, it was upsetting to find out that Isabella had talked to Adrian about it while she'd never once talked to *her*. That stung.

Isabella's admission turned into another one of those sad moments wrapping around Caprice, and she fought hard not to let it show as it wasn't Isabella's fault. It was part of the process of the give and take that went on between parent and child, much as she hated admitting it. "So, what did Adrian have to say?" she asked, taking great care to keep her voice steady.

"That he misses Sean like crazy."

"Sean?" Caprice questioned.

"His little boy. He's younger than me."

"Adrian has a son?" All the back and forth they'd had, and he'd never mentioned that he had a son? That stung, too. No real reason that it should, but it did.

"Sean is with his mother now," Isabella said, totally uninterested in this conversation already. She bent down to watch a small beetle scoot across the grass. Transfixed by it for only a moment, she lost interest, then stood back up and resumed her watch for another spider monkey.

"Isabella, did he say anything else about Sean?" She'd recognized the paternal instincts in him, seen the way he was so good with children, yet this… She couldn't describe her feelings, knowing he was more comfortable confiding in Isabella than her, especially when she'd thought…well, it didn't matter what she'd thought, did it? There wasn't anything between them. Nothing at all, and if she hadn't known that before, she certainly did now.

In a way it was ironic how she'd been the one insisting on no personal relationship, and now she was the one feeling the sting of knowing just how much he'd taken her at her word.

"No," Isabella said. "He didn't say nothing else."

"Anything," Caprice corrected. "Didn't say *anything* else."

"Except that I'm j-just like you. That's good, isn't it?"

Caprice smiled. "That's good, if you want to be like me." She wasn't sure that it really was, though. Somehow she thought her daughter deserved better. At least deserved the honesty to know more than she herself had the courage to tell her. And there were so many things she would have to tell her daughter one day. Not yet, but the day wasn't so far off. Adrian had said as much, and now she knew why. He'd spoken as a father would because he was a father. A secret, or a deliberate omission, that did hurt.

"Absolutely. P-positively, Dr Bona-ven-tura. I want to be j-just like you!"

Caprice laughed. "I absolutely, positively couldn't have said it better myself, Miss Isabella Bonaventura." Isabella and her big words. The child struggled so hard to use them, to pronounce them perfectly, to sound grown-up. She was so lucky to have Isabella. But what about Adrian and his son? What kind of relationship did they have? Did he have custody or was that one of the things he'd lost in his divorce? Was that the reason he hated women with issues?

In a way it all made sense, but what still didn't make sense was that she'd thrown herself at a man she didn't know at all, and more than that, she'd confided things to him she'd never said to anybody else. She'd been on the verge of turning her life upside down for a man who'd never once mentioned that he had a child of his own, which showed her how much he'd cared for her. More aptly put, did *not* care for her enough to tell her. Well, so much for the comfort of her own delusions. Adrian was the man who'd set off her warning hairs the very first time she'd seen him, and she should have stayed with that feeling.

Next time, she would.

Lesson learnt.

There would be no more men in her life. In one way or another, they were all worthless. Her father, her ex-husband… now Adrian.

"I'm glad you called," Ben said breathlessly. "My investigator has spotted Sylvie. She's in Miami now, staying in a residential hotel away from the beach. Kind of a low-scale place, but nothing that's going to harm Sean."

"Sean?" he asked anxiously. "Did he see him?"

"Yes, he saw him. Took a digital photo of him and he seems to be fine. Maybe a little tired, but overall not in bad condition, from what I could tell."

"Did he approach them? Did Sean say anything"

"No, I didn't want him to. Didn't think it wise."

He was probably right about that, but Adrian was bitterly disappointed. "I'm coming home," Adrian stated. "Today. Right now." This time he was going to do it. Nothing was going to talk him out of it.

"I'm not stopping you," Ben replied. "In fact, the sooner, the better. Apparently, she's moved around a few times. According to the manager of the hotel where she's staying right now, she only checked in there yesterday. Which means she was somewhere else before that. Who knows how often she moves?"

"She moves around so much because she knows I'm looking for her."

"Well, Paul Radke, the investigator, is watching the hotel as we speak. I told him not to lose track of her, so he's sitting across the street in a spot where he can see the hotel entrance. But I don't trust her, Adrian. Since she's moving around to avoid you finding her, she'll be moving again. *Soon.*"

"Then, like I said, I'm on my way." He hung up, ran back to his room, packed his belongings and went to talk to Grant Makela about buying a ride in Grant's borrowed plane to San José. If Grant wouldn't do it, somebody else would because money talked, and right now, before Sylvie got through with him, he still had some. Of course, that was today. But tomorrow?

Dr Lawrence Snowden was reading a mystery novel in the garden, stretched out and relaxed in a cabana chair, sipping on a soft drink, as Caprice walked by him on her way back to her afternoon surgery. "You got word about Adrian and this afternoon's surgical schedule?" she asked. Quite honestly, she was a little surprised that Lawrence wasn't gowning up already, but she didn't dictate the surgical procedures. She only outlined the schedules. So maybe he waited until the last minute, relaxing as he was now, right up until that time. In all honesty, with all the stress in her life, it didn't seem like such a bad thing to do.

Lawrence, a distinguished, gray-haired man in his late sixties, who hailed from Calgary, Alberta, nodded. "I was surprised about it, as this is going to drastically affect the entire schedule of the whole outfit, but I suppose it can't be helped, and I'm sure you've got it worked out to have someone come in right away to take his place."

"What?" Caprice gasped. "What are you talking about?"

"A replacement for Dr McCallan, now that he's left us. You do have one on the way, don't you?"

"What do you mean, he's left us?" It still wasn't sinking in.

"Twenty minutes ago one of the local ranchers with an airplane took him to San José. He asked Grant to fly him, but Grant was busy with a patient, and he referred him to someone on a coffee plantation near here. That's all I know, except that he was trying to make a connection back to Miami."

This couldn't be happening! *Absolutely could not be happening!* Sure, they'd had their little spat. But then he'd gone? Just like that, upped and left without a word to her. It didn't make sense. Of course, she'd be stupid to say she didn't believe it couldn't happen as that's what he'd tried to do right off, the minute he'd landed in Costa Rica. Hadn't he wanted to turn around and go right back home?

Well, apparently she was much more wrong about Dr Adrian McCallan than she was right, because she'd truly thought he would stay for the duration of his promise. The man was less than worthless, though. More than that, he was a complete bastard for putting the whole operation in a bind the way he was. That was unforgivable. Inconsiderate and totally unforgivable, and she had a good mind to go to San José after him to have a few words with him, the least of those being that he would never, ever be allowed to volunteer with any team from Operation Smiling Faces again once she got through filing her report.

"Is Grant busy now?" she asked Lawrence.

"Saw him heading to the cafeteria a few minutes ago."

She nodded. "Do me a favor. Take over the afternoon schedule as you were going to do. And ask one of the volunteers to postpone my cases. I had only one light one, and maybe we can work something out to get it onto another schedule or have one of the other anesthesiologists stand in for an extra procedure with me later tonight. Can you do that for me?"

Lawrence shut his book, took a sip of his drink, then stood. "And I suppose you want Grant to warm up the plane?"

"I suppose I do," she said, "as one of us is without an anesthesiologist and can't operate anyway." With that, she ran to catch up with Josefina, who was taking Isabella for an afternoon swim. She explained that she would be back by evening, then she went to meet Grant, who was snacking on a sandwich, sitting in the front seat of the truck, waiting to go to the landing strip. Apparently, Lawrence had waylaid him with the message.

"I would have taken Adrian to San José myself," Grant explained, "but I was checking on one of the children. She had a slight fever, and I wanted to get some antibiotics started since she's on the surgery schedule for day after tomorrow. I think I'm going to have to postpone her a few days."

"Schedule it any way you want," Caprice said. "As we're down one anesthesiologist, I don't know how the surgical rotation is going to work yet anyway."

"I'd heard. Tough break. Hope it doesn't set us back too much."

She nodded her agreement with that sentiment. "He didn't happen to tell you *why* he was leaving, did he?" As if she didn't know.

"Something personal was all he said. And I didn't ask any more."

Something personal! That struck a sour chord as *she'd* been that something personal. She'd pushed him away before they'd got involved personally, and he was doing the same. "Damn his *something personal,*" Caprice snapped. Blame him, blame her. Either way, it turned out the same.

Grant gave her a curious glance as he started the truck. Not another word was spoken until they reached the landing strip, and barely a word was spoken on the flight to San José, other than to discuss some of the various patients they had.

It was probably a silly thing to do, chasing after Adrian, she thought after they landed. Quite reactionary of her. Even over-reactionary, but wasn't that what she did, according to Adrian? Overreact? Well, she did have paperwork to complete, too…the documents he was supposed to sign in order to check himself out of the operation. She had slipped them into her bag alongside her own paperwork and passport, which she always carried with her. Technically, until that was accomplished, he was still part of it. OK, so that was merely a formality. Him walking away pretty much served the same purpose as the release document. But making it legal and official gave her the excuse she wanted to have the last word with Adrian McCallan.

She would pay for the flight herself and, for once, admit that it was something personal. Something *very* personal, only the way having the last word could be. Another over-reaction from Caprice Bonaventura, but she owed herself this one.

"I suppose I'll be waiting for you?" Grant called, as Caprice climbed out of the plane and started to head off across the tarmac.

"Won't be long," she called back. Just long enough to tell Adrian what she really thought of him. Problem was, what she really thought and what she wanted to say were two entirely different things. And she wasn't sure which would pop out.

"Ten minutes, and we'll be ready to go, sir," the private pilot told Adrian. "I'm going to go down and have a last check of the plane, then we'll call you to board."

Adrian nodded, looking out the window at the plane. Ben had secured the hire of a small private jet, which meant he really *did* want Adrian back home as fast as possible. He'd expected plane tickets on the next commercial flight out to Miami, but instead, when he'd called Ben from the airport, Ben had told him of the arrangements he'd already made. Not that Adrian was kicking about having a private plane all to himself, because he wasn't. But the implication that waiting an additional four hours to catch the next commercial flight going to Miami wasn't something Ben wanted him to do did concern him. Had the situation become more urgent and Ben was trying to downplay it? Could something have happened to Sean?

That last thought caused Adrian to draw in a sharp breath as a long list of grim possibilities crossed his mind. Illness, injury, emotional breakdown. Surely Sylvie wouldn't neglect him, would she? She was ruthless, and selfish, but he'd never thought her the type to be abusive. Of course, people changed, didn't they? Look at the way he'd changed once he'd had Sean in his life. Nobody but nobody would have ever guessed him the type to be a regular family man before that. But look at him now. His life was defined by his family. And was better for it.

But Sylvie… No! He wasn't going to think about her hurting Sean in any way. She would use him, and manipulate him, but she wouldn't harm him. He had to believe that, or his guilt over what was happening would crush him even more than it already had.

Still, as Adrian was called to board the plane and as he settled himself into the comfortable tan leather seat—the only one filled of the dozen in the airplane cabin—he couldn't help wondering about the urgency of this trip. Wonder, and worry.

A private jet? Adrian had boarded a private jet? "You've got to be kidding," Caprice snapped.

She stood by the terminal building, simply looking at the airplane. Fifteen minutes ago she'd been all brave and blustery and full of words she wanted to vent on Adrian, questions she wanted to ask. But now she wasn't sure. The Adrian she'd thought she'd known might have been worth her anger, but this one—she simply didn't know. Didn't trust him, didn't trust her feelings for him. She was too over-reactive, too hurt, too…much in love.

No, that couldn't be right! She couldn't be…

But if she wasn't, then why this trip to the airport, why the fury to run after him, have words with him?

It was better to let him go, really. Better to keep things as they had been before Adrian had come into her life. Better for both her and Isabella. She didn't need the headaches and heartaches. Didn't need…a man.

But she wanted one. More specifically she wanted Adrian. Which made that love, didn't it? She'd gone and done it and now he was throwing it back at her, using her own excuse.

What a fool she'd been! Total fool.

She deserved it, though. Anyone who went against personal dictates the way she'd done deserved what they got. So maybe all this anger should be vented at herself for not listening to herself.

Somehow, though, as she watched the plane, knowing he was inside, getting ready to fly out of her life, the anger melted, and all she could feel was…lonely again.

It was time to let him go, she decided. Let it be. Time to refocus on her mission here, go pick up a few medical supplies from the hospital to make her trip worthwhile. Time to return to Dulce, forget him, forget she'd even been attracted to him.

"I talked to the pilot," Grant said, stepping up behind her. "Their flight plan is filed and they're cleared for take-off in about ten minutes. If you have something to say to the man, I'd suggest you do it pretty fast, because the pilot's being paid some pretty hefty cash to get them back to Miami as quickly as possible."

"Miami," Caprice muttered.

"In nine minutes, and counting," Grant prompted.

"I shouldn't have come here," she said. "Stupid whim."

"Or maybe you should have. I've known you for a while, Caprice, and you're usually not given to impulses like this. I'm not going to pry into your personal affairs with this guy, but I have a hunch you're going to need some resolution here. And in eight minutes that opportunity's going to fly away. Oh, and for what it's worth, some whims are good."

Caprice looked at Grant. He was a nice man, a good friend and an excellent doctor. She had an idea his patients adored him, because she did. He was a vital part of this operation and a smart man. Also a perceptive one. "It was personal," she admitted.

"I'm not surprised. I knew it would happen to you someday."

"Not that. We weren't—"

"Doesn't matter what you weren't," he interrupted. "Or were. In seven minutes, whatever it was you were or weren't is going to Miami." He gave her a little nudge with his elbow. "Better go square it away with him, Caprice. One way or another, you've got to go take care of it, or you're going to regret it."

"It sounds like you're talking from experience."

Grant laughed. "Let's just say that I've had my fair share of experience with regrets, and leave it at that."

"Maybe you're right," she said, watching the pilot of Adrian's plane make his way around to the entry steps.

"You've got six minutes to find out. That pilot's stepping pretty lively, though, so it may be down to five."

"Five minutes," Caprice whispered, still not budging.

"It's not like you to back down, Caprice. I'm guessing you must really love the guy to be so hesitant."

Love the guy? Maybe that was the case, or maybe, when she was more clear-headed, she'd see it as one of her typical over-reactions. Whatever the case, right now she wanted to throttle the guy, and Grant's observation finally thrust her back to where she had been twenty minutes ago. There were a few, rather pointed, things she had to say to Adrian McCallan, no matter how she felt about him, and five minutes was plenty of time. "I'll be right back," she said, running out onto the tarmac to the jet, then up the entry steps.

"Adrian!" she snapped, stepping into the cabin.

He bolted out of his seat. "Caprice! What are you doing here?"

"I think the more appropriate question is, what are you doing here? We had an agreement—"

"Ready for take-off," the pilot said from the front of the cabin.

"Look, Caprice. I'll call you once I'm back in Miami. OK?"

"Sir, the tower has cleared us. We've got to leave," the pilot prompted.

"The problem is, you'll be back in Miami and I'll be stuck here without an anesthesiologist," she snapped, not budging.

"Get off the plane, Caprice," Adrian said, taking hold of her arm. But she jerked away from him.

"Why, Adrian? At least tell me that much. I have to know. Is it because of what I said this morning, that we couldn't—?"

"Sir, we either leave now or we're going to be delayed, and there's no guarantee how long it's going to be…"

"Caprice, we'll talk about it. I promise. But right now…" He made another try at her arm, but she stepped back.

"What about the children, Adrian? What am I supposed to tell them? That their doctor and anesthesiologist had *personal problems* that couldn't be resolved, so they're not getting their surgery? I thought you were better than that. I thought you would honor your promise to stay for the full two weeks."

"Sir, it's now, or we don't take off for at least an hour, according to the air controller. And there's a weather front on its way in, tropical storm, which could delay us well past that."

Adrian looked at Caprice, who was hell-bent on having her say. "You've got to go," he said evenly. "We'll talk about this once I land."

She set her shoulders stubbornly, and took two steps forward. "You have to sign out of Operation Smiling Faces. I have the papers…" As she started to unlatch her shoulder-bag, Adrian expelled an exasperated breath, then gave the nod to the pilot, who shut the door and took his place in his seat.

"I'm sorry, Caprice," he said. "I didn't want to do this."

Caprice didn't even notice that the plane was beginning to roll down the runway until she'd found the documents for Adrian to sign and looked up at him. "You're kidnapping me?" she choked.

"Not kidnapping. I asked you to leave, and you wouldn't. So now you're going to Miami. Like I said, I'm sorry. But you're stubborn. Wouldn't listen."

"Let me off this plane, Adrian! Right now. Tell the pilot to stop and let me out!"

He shook his head, then turned around and went back to his seat. "It's out of my hands," he said, once he was seated and belted in. "I'd suggest you pick a seat and buckle yourself in, too, because we're not turning back. It's too late."

"You can't do this!"

"You did it to yourself, Caprice." Having her along might have been nice under different circumstances, but somehow he didn't think anything about this trip was going to be nice. Not in any form. Going from one woman who now hated him straight to another who'd hated him for years... Adrian leaned back in the seat, shut his eyes, exhaled a weary sigh, and vowed to himself that he wouldn't open his eyes again until he was back on the ground. It was an evasion tactic, he knew, but sometimes a little evasion didn't hurt.

Back on the tarmac, Grant Makela visored his eyes with his hand to blot out the sun. "Hmm," he said, shaking his head as he the plane disappeared into the clouds. With Caprice still inside. "She must be in love to do something like that."

CHAPTER NINE

THE first part of the flight took place in absolute silence. He feigned sleep, even tried to sleep, but it wasn't happening. His mind was exploding with too many things—Sean, Caprice's problems, the feelings he had going on for Caprice in spite of the fact he didn't want them to.

He tried concentrating on the low drone of the jet engines for the first little while, but that merely turned irritating as he thought about how long it was taking to get back home, get back to his son. Then he tried concentrating on work and, naturally, Caprice came to mind. With Caprice came all her problems…problems he tried to convince himself weren't any of his business. But then his feelings for Caprice changed his mind on that one because caring for her meant taking on her problems, and he did care for her, crazy as that was.

Of course, taking on her problems circled him right back to Sean and the problem Sylvie had caused for both of them, which circled him even further back to his original vow not to get involved with a woman who had issues. Issues… That took him around the circle one more time, stopping at Caprice. All this going around in circles gave him a headache and a good reason not to open his eyes.

But she was so quiet, and he was tempted to take a look at the back of the cabin, where she'd settled in, to see what she was doing. Fuming, for sure. That couldn't be helped. He'd told her to get off and she hadn't, and he hadn't been about to miss his window of opportunity to leave for Miami, especially with Ben making it so clear that his presence back there, immediately, was important enough to warrant hiring a private jet. To be perfectly blunt about it, Caprice's stubbornness had got her here. She wouldn't see it that way, but that's the way it was. In time, he would apologize. Not now, though. Not until that greatest share of her anger had abated a little.

All these thoughts and problems compounded the headache, and right now any overture toward Caprice, good, bad, apologetic or otherwise, would compound it even more. Sure, it would have been nice having her here under different circumstances. A quick little trip to Miami for the night. Dining, dancing. Making love in the wee hours. That's the way he would have preferred this to have worked out. But with Caprice as an unwilling guest…

Adrian cringed with regret over that one, then stood and went forward to the pilot to make amends, if that were at all possible. It was the very least he could do as, contrary to the way it looked, he didn't want to inconvenience Caprice, or make her life harder. She had so many things to deal with. But so did he, and this was a chance he couldn't miss. Wouldn't miss, no matter how much he regretted what he'd just been forced to do.

Two minutes later he was back in the cabin, standing in the aisle, looking at the very last seat, where Caprice was turned toward the window, one leg crossed over the other, simply staring out. She was already missing Isabella, probably worried out of her mind. Worried about Operation Smiling Faces, too.

Headache or not, he did have to apologize now. At least make the attempt. He owed her that much even if she wasn't yet ready to be receptive. "I'm sorry about this," he finally said. "This isn't what I wanted to happen."

She said nothing. Neither did she turn to look at him.

"I asked you to get off, you know. You did hear the pilot say we had to take off and I asked you, Caprice. More than once. You wouldn't leave. And whether or not you believe this, I didn't keep you here, and I didn't want to take you along unwillingly. All that said, I really am sorry about this."

She turned even more toward the window, effectively giving him the cold shoulder.

"I know you're worried about Isabella, but I've had the pilot call ahead and reserve you a ticket to San José, so you'll be back there tonight. It's taken care of, no expense to you or Operation Smiling Faces, and I'm sure Grant Makela will take care of informing Josefina, so Isabella will be fine." Someone had taken his son away from him, and now he was taking someone's mother away from her. He felt terrible about it. Felt terrible about the way things were turning out all the way round. This wasn't what he'd had in mind when he'd started the journey to Costa Rica. Or even started the day. "You can take her a present," he said, grasping at straws now.

That one got a response from her. Caprice turned around enough to stare him down, then said, "And what, exactly, do you propose I take as a present? Those little packages of peanuts and crackers from the airplane? Sample snacks to make up for the fact that her mother went flying off without so much as kissing her goodbye?"

"Look, I didn't mean this to happen. All I wanted was to go home. Not to drag you along with me. But you didn't give me another choice, Caprice. I had to get out of there when I had the opportunity."

"You couldn't have waited that extra hour for a new clearance, or until after the storm had passed? Were you in such a hurry to get away from me that even a short delay was out of the question?"

"That's what you thought? That I was trying to get away from you?"

"What else could I think? After what I said to you this morning…" She shook her head in frustration. "I'm used to men running away, Adrian. I can deal with it. But not from Operation Smiling Faces. Not when I was the cause of those personal problems, and I know that I was. We could have worked through it. Kept both a personal and professional distance, if that's what it would have taken. But you simply left. And didn't even do me the courtesy of telling me."

"You were busy," he said.

"And you were in too much of a hurry."

"I'm not denying it. I had to leave, had to get home as fast as I could. But I wasn't running away from you, Caprice. This wasn't about you, or us. I have personal problems."

"Easy the way you can use that as an excuse," she snapped. "Easy the way you failed to mention that you have a son. Oh, it was fine for me to get personal with you, to…to tell you things I've never told anybody, to trust you when I knew better. But you didn't think enough of me to tell me anything about your life, about your son. I had to hear it from my eight-year-old daughter."

"Because she doesn't have such an aversion to getting personal." This wasn't going to work, no matter what he said. She was damn mad. And she certainly had that right. No point standing here arguing about it, rehashing things done and not done. He'd made his apologies, she had not accepted them, and that's the way it was going to be for now. He'd try again later, after his life was normal again. When his emotions weren't so volatile.

Adrian studied Caprice for a moment before he returned to his seat. One thing was for sure. Anger became the lady. He'd never seen her looking sexier. Fine time to be thinking about that. She would just as soon throw him out the door without a parachute while he'd just as soon join her at the back of the cabin and take her up on her offer from the other night.

Fat chance. She wasn't budging, and even if she did, he wasn't sure that she *wouldn't* throw him out that door anyway.

If there was one thing that was certain in all this, it was that Caprice Bonaventura was stubborn. She was annoying and frustrating and sexier than anything he could imagine, as testified by the erection straining at the zipper of his khakis. Time to sit down, think about less provocative things, he decided.

When Adrian was back in his seat, though, the harder he tried not thinking about Caprice, the more he thought about her. Even after he shut his eyes again and tried listening to the drone of the jet engine, the only thing playing through his mind was Caprice.

OK, so technically he wasn't kidnapping her. She understood that. He'd asked her to get off and she hadn't. That stubborn streak in her and all. So an unexpected trip to Miami was the consequence. Still, he didn't have to do this. And, yes, he was right that she was worried about Isabella. Her daughter was in excellent hands, but that wasn't the point. The point was, she didn't want to be here. Couldn't be here. She had responsibilities back at Dulce and even half a day away made a huge impact.

Of course, once she was back she would still be down one surgical team and perhaps that was the biggest point of all. Adrian had compromised so many facets of the operation. He'd reduced the number of surgeries they could perform, he'd put off patients who might have to wait until she returned in another three months for their surgeries, he'd disrupted so many lives that had counted on Operating Smiling Faces.

Truthfully, she'd let down her guard. She's gotten personal with him, allowed her feelings to take over. Even been so stupid as to tell him her feelings. And what did she get for it all? An impromptu airplane ride to Miami.

"So if you're not leaving because of me…" she started, then stopped. What was the point? She'd only get in deeper.

"I have a son," he admitted, his voice almost a whisper. She thought she heard pain there, and it startled her. Did he truly have family problems? Perhaps something about the son he'd failed to mention to her?

Suddenly all the anger drained right out of her. "Is this trip about him?" she asked, unfastening her seat belt and standing. Caprice moved forward and stopped next to Adrian's seat. "There's something more than you missing him so badly you have to go home, isn't there?"

The anguish coming from Adrian was so intense she could almost feel it.

He looked up at her but didn't say a word. His eyes spoke volumes, though. In them she saw overwhelming sadness… sadness she recognized when she was worried so much over Isabella that the emotional pain turned into a physical one. "Am I really that self-involved?" she asked. "Do I seem that way to you, Adrian? Too self-involved to care that you're going through something terribly wrong? Too self-involved that you won't even tell me what it is, to let me try to help?"

"What are you talking about, Caprice?" His voice was impatient, edgy.

"I'm wondering if your impression of me is that I don't care about your problems or about what's going on in your life." She feared that it might be, hoped that it wasn't, but understood if it was. She did get too wrapped up in staying un-personal. She knew that. It kept her safe. Protected her.

"No," he said, shutting his eyes and leaning his head against the headrest again. "That's not the way I see you."

"Then why didn't you ever talk to me?"

"And tell you what? That while I was on my way to Costa Rica my ex-wife was taking my son and holding him for what would appear to some as a ransom? How does that make me look, Caprice? Negligent? Self-involved myself? Uncaring? A total incompetent as a father?"

Caprice sat down in the seat across from Adrian, facing him. "She took him without court approval?" she gasped.

"I have full custody. She has visitation rights, that's all. Which she never uses unless she wants more money from me."

"You gave the woman money when she doesn't have custody?" She herself had waived support payments from Tony because she didn't want the tie to him. So what Adrian had done—paid support to a woman who hadn't been awarded it by the court—did cause her to wonder. The man should have felt so much spite towards his ex-wife, yet he'd tried to be fair. Adrian was a man of great concern.

That caused her feelings for him to deepen.

"I give the woman money and she leaves the two of us alone to lead reasonably normal lives in the times between. Normal, until she shows up the next time."

Caprice was horrified. All the time she'd been crying on his shoulder about her problems, he had been suffering over a son gone missing. "I'm so sorry, Adrian," she choked out in a broken whisper. "So sorry. I had no idea—"

"He's safe," Adrian interrupted, finally twisting in his seat to look at her. "Sylvie's bad in a lot of ways, but she'd never hurt Sean."

"You're sure of that?"

He nodded. "For her it's all about the money. She'll do what it takes to get my every last penny, but she won't hurt Sean. Just use him."

"But that's hurting him," Caprice said, on the verge of tears for the pain Adrian had to be suffering. She couldn't even begin to imagine what she'd do if Tony suddenly came back into their lives and took Isabella away. It would kill her. Literally kill her.

"Don't you think I know that?" he snarled. Finally, he

turned to face her fully. "She'll feed him and make sure he's safe. But what kind of a mother would put her child in the position she has Sean?"

Not a mother, Caprice thought. Adrian's wife was not a mother in any sense of the word. "You'd just found out when you arrived, hadn't you? That's why you wanted to go right back home that first day."

"That's why, and I would have but my attorney advised me there was nothing I could do. He thought I was better off staying away, which would keep me out of his way as he tried to find Sean. He was afraid I would make matters worse."

"That had to be rough," she said, her voice full of sympathy. "I don't think I could have stayed out of it if the same thing happened to Isabella. I understand the need to keep you away, but I'm sorry he did, Adrian."

He turned his head to study her for a moment, but didn't say a word. So she did, to break the awkward, sad silence between them. "Sean," Caprice said. "Sean McCallan. Nice name. Do you have a picture?"

Adrian looked surprised for a moment, then pulled his wallet from his pocket and flipped it open to a color photo of a little boy playing on a swing. Red, curly hair, lots of freckles, mischievous green eyes, a little bit of baby fat still lingering in all the right baby fat places…nothing like Adrian, but just about the cutest little thing she'd ever seen. "He's adorable!" she exclaimed.

He nodded dryly, then snapped the wallet shut. "I never expected her to do this," he said. "She's spent most of his life ignoring him, then she waited until the first time I've left him for any considerable amount of time to take him."

"And you're feeling guilty, blaming yourself, saying things to yourself you don't deserve."

"Damn right I am. If I'd—"

She leaned across and laid a hand on his knee. "No recriminations, Adrian. You didn't know, couldn't know. And if you had, you wouldn't have let this happen. It wasn't your fault."

"Tell that to my son," he snapped.

"He knows you love him, Adrian. That's what he trusts. That's all he needs to trust."

"All he trusts until I betrayed that trust."

"But you didn't. It was his mother, wasn't it? She's the one who betrayed him."

"I should have seen it."

"And I should have seen how cruel Tony would be to Isabella, but I kept hoping I was wrong, or that something in him would change. You can't beat yourself up because you couldn't predict this. And you can't think you get the blame for something that was so totally out of your control, because you don't. We all have blind spots, Adrian. That's not a fault. More like vulnerability."

"Vulnerability that made my child vulnerable."

"But he's been found?" she asked hopefully. "And he's OK?"

"He's been spotted by my private investigator and, according to the preliminary report, he's fine."

"Not the police?" she asked. "Because if this is a case of parental kidnapping—"

"No police," he snapped. "And it's not kidnapping in the real sense of the word. All that aside, even if it could legally be considered kidnapping, I don't want Sean thinking that his mother is a kidnapper. He doesn't need that."

"But, Adrian—"

He gave his head an angry shake, effectively stopping her. "No police," he repeated, this time quietly. "Like I said, I don't want my son involved in that kind of mess, and if we did call in the authorities they'd drag him into it."

She did understand that. When she and Tony had separated, then divorced, they'd taken great care to keep the whole situation entirely away from Isabella. Of course, Tony had been glad to be rid of his daughter however it happened, and Caprice doubted even a financial incentive could have forced him to want Isabella back in his life for any reason. "I still wish you'd said something. I mean, I understand you staying in Costa Rica…"

"Well, that makes one of us, because I sure as hell don't. It was a good argument at the time, and my attorney certainly did convince me it was in Sean's best interests that I stayed away while he handled the investigation. But in the end Sean is my son and I should have gone home, should have been looking for him myself."

"Look, I've experienced every kind of guilt you can imagine over Isabella, but one thing I learnt along time ago is that sometimes a parent's best intentions really aren't in the best interests of the child."

He blinked, and a slight smile tweaked at his lips. "Did I hear you right? You, the most over-protective parent I've ever known, are admitting that?"

"OK, so I talk a better game than I play, but it's true, and you're the one who's been pointing that out to me these past few days."

"And you actually listened," he said. The tension in his shoulders lessened a bit. "I've been really pompous, giving you parenting advice when my skills aren't exactly the best."

"I'll bet you're a great father. I've seen it in the way you were with Isabella and the other children. In fact, I should have guessed you had some experience other than professional, as natural as you are with them."

"I try to be a good father, but whether or not I am remains to be seen. At least you know where your daughter is. And I am sorry I took you away from her. I was frantic to get into the air. If I'd been thinking straight, I'd have thrown you over my shoulder and carried you off the plane."

Caprice smiled. "Somehow you don't strike me as the caveman type." The airplane took a bit of a dip as it pushed into the rough edge of the promised storm. Caprice gasped, grabbing the arms of her seat. "I really hate flying," she said, her knuckles going white as the plane dipped again. "Almost as much as flying hates me."

"Airsick?"

She bit down on her lip, nodding. "Most of the time I take Dramamine. Didn't have any warning for this trip. Thought I was going to make it through to Miami, but…" The plane lurched to the left and Caprice slid halfway to the floor.

"Trade seats," Adrian said, unbuckling. "That's a single. Mine's a double. You can stretch out." He stood, then helped her to her feet. Just as she teetered up, though, the plane hit another little air pocket and she fell straight into Adrian's arms.

"I'm not really throwing myself at you like I did the other night," she said, making no attempt to extricate herself from the arms locking tight around her. "I only do that once in a relationship. You had your chance."

He chuckled. "As green as your face is right now, I'm really not thinking along those lines."

"Good thing," she said, looking up at him. Truth was, even with the queasiness overtaking her, she *was* thinking along those lines. It didn't take much to get it started either. Just minutes ago she had been ready to kill him but now, nausea notwithstanding, she was ready to pull him down into the seat with her and see what the good doctor could do at this elevation. Had she popped a Dramamine before the flight, she might have found out. Told Adrian it was what the doctor ordered to take his mind off his problems. But she hadn't taken an airsick pill, nothing was going to take Adrian's mind off his missing son, and, to be honest, the thought of any excess movement of any kind made the nausea worse. So, regrettably, Caprice pulled herself out of Adrian's hold and tumbled down into his seat.

For the next several minutes Caprice turned inward, trying to distract herself from the growing nausea, the increasing awareness of her feelings for Adrian, and the bitter despair of knowing that they weren't a good fit. That, as well as the fact she still didn't want *that kind* of relationship in her life. Then finally, as the airplane's rocking and rolling evened out, she managed to relax a little and turn her thoughts outward again. "Why didn't you tell me about him, Adrian? Not about the fact that your ex-wife took him but that you had a son?" He was stretched out in the seat across from her, positioned so they were face to face. Casual, in spite of the turmoil in his life. Worry lines were etched deeply into his face, yet his concerned eyes were on her, and that concern was for her. He was a man of so many depths, most of which she probably hadn't discovered. And the ones she had discovered she liked. Even admired.

"It's not an easy thing to answer, but I think, putting it into simple terms, I try to keep that part of my life private. Like you, I compartmentalize. I don't take my son to work, don't take my work home to my son. He's always in my heart, but for me to function the way I need to for everybody depending on me, I can't blur the lines. I mean, I was a man who truly never thought about having children, about having the kind of commitment and responsibilities I have now. Then one day he was there and everything changed."

"For the better?" she asked.

"In ways I can't even put into words. And the thing is, it's always been just the two of us. My mother steps in to help but day in, day out it's just us guys and for this guy, it's been easier to compartmentalize my life. So why didn't I mention I had a son? It wasn't what going to Costa Rica was about. I wasn't there to make friends, get personal. Kind of like you, I suppose. On top of that, with this situation with Sylvie going on…" He shrugged. "It seemed easier. Then after we became friends, and even flirted with involvement, you already had so many issues that you simply didn't need to be involved in mine. And you did put up so many walls. But it wasn't that I didn't trust you as much as I didn't trust me to keep your boundaries. Which, by the way, were pretty much like my own boundaries. Although it's easier to see them and criticize them in someone else. Especially when they're starting to slip in yourself. And mine were slipping, Caprice. You were causing them to slip."

"So I was a convenient excuse?" She laughed.

"Something like that."

Well, that's something she certainly understood because in so many ways that's how she lived her life. Not wanting friends, not getting personal… But it didn't feel so good, being on the receiving end as she was. Being pushed away instead of pushing…

Suddenly Caprice was filled with regret for so many things she might have pushed away in her life. Things, people, relationships she might have trusted. "So, when you and your wife had Sean…" she started, trying to get off the topic of regrets.

Adrian shifted impatiently in his seat, his body going from casual to rigid.

Bad topic, she thought. Really bad topic.

"What I didn't plan on was having a wife."

That much said, he didn't continue, and Caprice wondered if she should simply let it go or probe a little further. He clearly wasn't comfortable with this topic, and now that the tension between them had finally lifted, she decided it best to let it go. If he wanted to talk, he would, and she would listen. That's what a friend would do. If he didn't, she'd close her eyes and take a nap. That's what a friend would do, too, even though she wanted to be more than a friend to him. He didn't want that from her, though. It was obvious. She'd burnt that bridge too badly to expect a repair. Couldn't blame him. But it hurt.

Another minute elapsed without a word from Adrian, so Caprice opted for settling in with a blanket that had been over the back of the seat, pulling her legs up and finding a fairly comfortable, semi-reclining position. There was still some time to go before they reached Miami so she may as well make herself comfy, since this, added to the trip right back home, was going to make for an awfully long time in the air.

Shutting her eyes, she listened to Adrian breathing. It was short and sharp. He was still thinking about his wife. Or maybe thoughts of Sean were haunting him again. Perhaps both.

He was a man with his own torments, own issues. No wonder he didn't want a woman with issues…a woman with so many issues of her own she didn't think she could deal with his problems, too. That made her sad. Sad deep to her soul because she wasn't like that at all. But she'd never given him cause to see that.

It was almost ten minutes before Adrian spoke again, and when he did her eyes flew open. She hadn't been sleeping. More like lost in her thoughts…Isabella, Tony, even Sean. And most of all Adrian.

"I went out with her once," he said.

"Your wife?"

Adrian nodded. "One evening, one night. I'd had a bad day and that's all I wanted with her. She was gone in the morning and I honestly forgot about her. Back in those days I wasn't the gentleman you accused me of being." He smiled. "In fact, you're the first person to ever say that about me. But the bottom line is, I slept with Sylvie that one time, and seven months later she was back on my doorstep, seven months pregnant. So I did the honorable thing by marrying her."

"That sounds pretty gentlemanly to me."

"Believe me, it wasn't. But I had a child coming into the world and I wanted to do the right thing, which was marrying my child's mother and trying to make a decent home. So that's I did, and we had a rather strained relationship before Sean was born. There are a lot of things to fill your time when you're expecting a baby, though, so we got through by spending our days buying baby clothes, our evenings preparing a baby room, our nights sleeping separately. Time went by pretty fast, and it wasn't horrible. Wasn't good either, but I don't think I ever had the expectation that it would be, or even should be. No matter as, after a while, Sean came along.

"He was born with an obstructed bowel and needed surgery when he was a couple of days old. It wasn't a complicated procedure and I wasn't worried, but the hospital was a little low on blood at that point so, of course, I volunteered to donate mine. Except Sean's type didn't match mine. So Sylvie went to donate hers. But they wouldn't take it."

Adrian stopped again, and ran his fingers through his hair. "Age-old story. Her type didn't match Sean's either."

Caprice gasped. "He's not…"

Adrian shook his head. "He's not mine. In the biological sense, anyway."

"I don't know what to say. Did Sylvie know?"

"She said she didn't. But with a woman like Sylvie, who knows? Didn't matter anyway. Sean already had my name, and the first time I looked at him that sealed the deal for me. I was his father. No turning back. I wanted to be his dad. I wanted him to be my son."

"And Sylvie?"

"She didn't care as long as there was support money involved. She walked out on us when Sean was eight months old. Didn't want any part of marriage or babies by then, and I was glad to see her go. She treated him…not badly. Not badly as much as indifferently. She didn't change diapers often enough, didn't feed him when he needed it, didn't do the things a mother would do— pick him up when he cried, play with him, sing to him when he fell asleep. And if there was something that could be put off until I got home, it was. I think I knew I wasn't going to stay married to her by the time Sean was a month old, but part of me kept hoping things would change. That blind spot you mentioned."

He paused, shaking his head sadly, regrettably. "I was busy in my career, with more and more opportunities opening up for me. I kept horrible hours and having a marriage seemed the best way to take care of things, to make sure Sean was cared for. At least, in my mind that's what I kept telling myself." He shrugged. "My heart was saying something else altogether. It was saying I'd hung on way too long with Sylvie. Of course, I wasn't listening. Then, one day, I came home and found Sean all alone. He'd been there alone for hours, while Sylvie was out shopping, or doing whatever it was that she did. Later, I found out that she'd left him alone before, and I blew up. She left. And she was glad to go."

"That's what you really wanted?"

"Honestly, I don't know what I wanted. The only thing I knew for sure was that Sean needed better than what he had for a mother, and as his father I had to protect him."

"She didn't want to take him with her?"

"She didn't even ask. I think, though, she knew I wouldn't allow it."

"I wonder if she knows how much she's missing?" Caprice asked.

"Sean's a great kid, but I don't suppose she does know, or she wouldn't be doing what she is."

"Not Sean," Caprice said, her voice lowering. "You. I wonder if she knows how much she's missing when it comes to you." Caprice slid further down into her seat, pulled the blanket up a little more, then shut her eyes. The nausea was gone now, as was her anger. As she drifted off to sleep she was filled with entirely new feelings for Adrian. Physical attraction had dictated her feelings up to this point, but now that was being edged out by something different, something more. She *was* in love with this man. For sure! She didn't want it, couldn't have it, but that didn't change facts. She was in love with Adrian McCallan in a way she'd never loved anyone else.

Falling in love again was something she'd never counted on. Falling in love with a man like Adrian made her realize just how much she didn't deserve him, and how much her heart would break when she couldn't have him.

And she couldn't because, when all was said and done, he would still hate women with issues…for good reason. But she was a woman with issues that weren't going to go away just because she recognized them and wanted them to. Therein was the problem, and there wasn't a fix.

CHAPTER TEN

"She thinks it's an adventure," Caprice said, after a ten-minute chat with Isabella. "Josefina's going to take her to her house for the rest of the day and night, and Isabella loves it there. It's in the jungle." A sad smile crossed her face. "Isabella said I could stay longer, if I wanted to."

Adrian chuckled, as he slung his bag into the back of the turquoise taxi cab. "Well, you've got to admire her honesty. Children have a way of being more blunt than we'd like sometimes." He turned around to face Caprice. "Are you sure you don't want to stay tonight, get some rest, and go back in the morning?"

Caprice shook her head. "I can't make it back to Dulce tonight, but at least I'll be closer to it if I'm in San José." She reached out and squeezed his hand. "I'm sorry about your son, Adrian. And I'm sorry I haven't always been very nice to you. If you want to come back to the operation some time, I'd like that. You're a good doctor."

With a weary sigh he pulled Caprice into his arms. "I'm sorry, too, about a lot of things." She felt so good there. Felt better than anyone ever had, and he didn't want to lose this. But he didn't know how to make it work. Or even make it start. There were too many obstacles right now, and there was no way he could plan into the future when his present wasn't figured out. First things first, then see what happens. "Maybe, after Sean is settled back in and I get some of our legal problems straightened out, we'll both come and spend a couple weeks with you in Costa Rica. But I'm not leaving him behind again. If I don't get full custody, and I can't get permission to let him travel with me…"

Caprice tilted her head up to him. "I understand," she whispered. "It's what I would do under the same circumstances."

Adrian lowered his face, pausing briefly before the inevitable kiss. "You could have made me change my mind about the kind of woman I want, Caprice," he said, his voice low.

She smiled. "You could have made me change my mind, too, but we have so many conflicts in our lives right now, Adrian. Conflicts that are more important than anything we want."

"Just for now let's not have those conflicts," he said, as he lowered his lips to hers. The kiss was tender at first, the feel of her delicate against him. The perfume of her hair wafted up to him…a flowery fragrance that would always remind him of Caprice. And the touch of her skin as he lifted his hands to cup her face…he would never feel skin so soft again in his life.

As the kiss turned from soft to seeking, he pulled her closer, desperation plain in the harder press of their lips and the way she wove her fingers behind his neck and clutched him in their embrace. He delved into her mouth with his tongue, seeking hers, and when he'd found it, it elicited a moan from him. And from her. Which strengthened the voracity of the kiss, strengthened the hold they had on each other. Instinctively, Adrian's hands moved to wrap around Caprice, then slowly slid down her back, but when they reached the delicate curve at the end of the journey, the kiss ended, and mutually they stepped away from each other.

For a moment, neither said a word. Then Adrian cleared his throat, breaking the hold of the moment. "I, um…I need to get going."

Caprice nodded.

"I'll call you," he said.

She nodded again.

"You've got all my phone numbers, so call me and let me know when you get back." He didn't want to leave her. Not for even a moment. "And if you need anything." To know someone for such a short time…someone who was so wrong for him…and to have these feelings for her, the way he was… "I'll see if I can find an anesthesiologist to send down to you, and I'll let you know one way or another by tomorrow." He loved her. That's all it could be. He was in love with Caprice Bonaventura. Issues and all, he was totally in love with the lady. Which, in itself, was a brand-new issue.

"And you'll let me know the minute you find Sean?" she asked.

He nodded, too shocked by his own realization to speak.

"It's almost time to leave, and they're not going to wait for me if I'm late," she said.

"Caprice, I—"

She stepped forward and put a finger to his lips to silence him. "No words, Adrian. Not now. We'll have time later." With that, she stood on tiptoe, gave him a quick, sweet kiss, then turned and ran back into the terminal.

Adrian watched her disappear into the crowds inside before he climbed into his own cab. Shakespeare may have once said that parting was such sweet sorrow, but there was nothing sweet about this. Not a damn thing!

"She's in there?" Adrian asked, his binoculars trained on the rundown motel across the street from where he, Ben, and Paul Radke were sitting in a black car.

"Haven't seen her leave," Paul said. "I've been here, or had one of my operatives here since I spotted her, and she hasn't come out."

The building was a two-story, white-painted stucco, with pink rails along the steps and upstairs walkways. Each room fronted on the street where they were sitting, and each pink door opened to the outside. There were no internal halls into which any doors opened. At the bottom, on the left, the glass-fronted office was obscured by a drive-through overhang where guests would park while they checked in. The motel wasn't a palace, more like a cheap sleep for a night or two, with lumpy mattresses and warm air-conditioning.

It was also the place where Sean was staying, which made Adrian anxious to go over there, knock on the door and, if not kick it in, take him away from Sylvie. "When do we go?" he asked, gripping the car door handle.

"Let me do the talking," Ben warned. "Do you understand me, Adrian? Not a word from you!"

"Not a word," Adrian agreed, grudgingly. Ben was right. He would be too reactive, and that could affect Sean. He had so many things he wanted to say to Sylvie, so much bitterness to vent over what she'd done, but for the sake of his son he would heed Ben's warning. As tough as that was going to be. "Not a word," he muttered again.

With that, the three men exited the car and marched, shoulder to shoulder, across the street. Paul was first up the stairs, followed by Ben, then Adrian. They marched in single file down the open walkway and stopped outside room 211. Paul was the one to knock, three loud bangs on the metal door, as Ben took care to keep himself between Adrian and the door.

No one answered, so Paul knocked again. This time louder.

Again, no answer, which caused Paul to pull out a cellphone and dial a number. He stepped away from the door and turned his back to the other two men, and in less than a minute he turned back to face them. "She's gone," he said. "According to the motel clerk, the maid said the room was empty earlier when she went to clean it. Apparently, she skipped out without paying the bill some time this afternoon."

Hearing those words, Adrian didn't say a thing. But he did shove past Ben and try the door. It was locked. So he took a step back, braced himself, raised his right leg and kicked it open. As the lock snapped and the door broke open, Adrian strode inside, took one look around, then strode back out and handed Ben a wad of bills to pay the manager for the damage. Adrian didn't ask how she'd gotten out without being seen, didn't ask why the investigator hadn't spotted her. It didn't matter. Gone was gone. This was Sylvie after all. She had her ways. And, last night she'd used them.

OK, so she hadn't hurried quite as much as she should have. The weather report in San José hadn't exactly encouraged her to catch the plane back either. Storms throughout the evening and into the night. Not severe storms but bad enough she didn't want to fly through them. So here she was, stepping out of the cab in front of the address Adrian had given her, wondering if she really should intrude on the father-son reunion.

They probably needed this time alone but, still, she felt compelled to be there—to have more time with Adrian, to meet his son. "Here," she said, giving the taxi driver his fare. "And some extra. Would you mind waiting for a few minutes, until I know whether or not I'll be staying?"

The taxi driver took a look at the money she'd handed over, decided the extra she'd included was sufficient for a short wait, and nodded. So with that Caprice made her way up the stone walk to the Spanish-style home, its porchlight glowing a bright yellow against the black of the night, and she knocked on massive Moorish-carved door. In only a second or two a man she didn't recognize answered the door.

"May I help you?" he asked, his voice flat.

"I thought this was Adrian McCallan's home," she said, noting the strain showing on the man's face.

"It is. May I tell him who's calling?"

"Caprice Bona—"

"Dr Bonaventura," the man interrupted, his voice showing more animation now. He extended his hand to her. "It's good to meet you. I'm Ben Rafferty, Adrian's attorney."

As she took his hand, her breath caught in her throat. This didn't seem right. No happiness here, like she'd expected. Had something happened to Sean? "What's wrong?" she asked in response.

"Not good news. Sean wasn't there. We went to get him but they were gone."

"How's Adrian?" she asked.

"Not good."

"Could I see him?"

Ben nodded, stepping aside. "He's taking it pretty hard. Hasn't really said much for the past couple of hours. Mostly, he's just pacing." He indicated the door to the study. It was closed. "He's in there. Doesn't want to be bothered, but I think he'll want to see you."

She wondered what Adrian had said about her to his attorney, but didn't ask. "I'll go and talk to him," she said, not sure what she could say to help. Words, in a situation such as this, couldn't possibly be enough.

"Good, then I think I'll go. He won't want both of us here, and I'd like to go and talk to the investigator to see if we can figure out what happened, and where we look next."

"Is Sean…?" She didn't know how to phrase this. "There wasn't anything to indicate he's been hurt, was there?"

"No. I don't think Sylvie would do that. More like she's trying to wear Adrian down. After what happened, I'm afraid it's beginning to work." He stepped to the door. "Tell him I'll call him later."

"Tell the cabbie not to wait," she said.

Ben nodded, then he left, pulling the door closed after him.

Caprice hesitated after the click, not sure what to say, what to do. She'd hesitated to come here because she hadn't wanted to interrupt a happy homecoming for Adrian and Sean. But this wasn't what she'd expected. Wasn't what Adrian had expected either, and all she could do was imagine how she would feel in the same situation.

She didn't even look at the furnishings in the contemporary interior as she approached the study door, didn't notice the pictures of Sean that were sitting on the glass coffee-table or the pictures of Adrian and Sean atop the bookshelf. This was too difficult, she was too nervous to notice anything. Even as she raised her hand to knock she wavered a moment, wondering if she should. Perhaps Adrian preferred going through this alone. Maybe the intrusion of an outsider was the last thing he wanted.

But if this were her…she'd want Adrian there. In her heart that was the only thing she knew for sure. She'd need his comfort. In the end, that's what caused her to knock. Softly. Then she stepped back to wait.

"Ben?" he called, his voice muffled through the door.

"No, it's me. Caprice."

There was no response, but seconds later the door opened to a black room…black but for the single dim bulb burning over the desk on the opposite side. "Ben told me what happened, and I'm so sorry, Adrian." His face was contorted in a way she'd never seen. A mix between anger and frustration, with a twinge of sadness. She studied him for a moment, then stepped into the room.

"Why are you here?" he asked, his voice thick.

"The weather is causing flights to be delayed and cancelled. I won't be able to fly back until morning. You'd given me your address… If you'd rather I go…"

Adrian shook his head. "No. That's not necessary." He stepped away, turned his back, then simply stood there. "We got there, she was gone. Left some time in the afternoon."

"Ben said he thinks that Sean is OK. At least that part is good," she said, trying to be encouraging, even though there was little to be encouraged about when your child was missing.

"How can a child be OK when someone like Sylvie is dragging him around?" He walked away from her to the opposite side of the room, then dropped down into a leather easy chair. "He needs to be home now," he said, his voice much too calm, much too quiet.

"Adrian, can I do something for you? Get you something to eat or drink?" Caprice asked. "Make phone calls? Anything?"

"I'm glad you're here," he said, trying to smile. "But there's nothing to do except wait."

"Then I'll wait with you."

"I appreciate that, but you have other responsibilities, Caprice. This isn't your problem."

He was trying to push her away, but she wasn't going to be pushed so easily. Right now Operation Smiling Faces was running quite nicely. Grant Makela was assuming the role of temporary director until she returned. Isabella was more than happy to stay with Josefina. So, it seemed, the only place she needed to be was here. Adrian shouldn't be going though this alone. She didn't want him to. "Not for a while," she said, walking slowly over to him. Instead of taking a seat at the desk adjacent to him, or in the other easy chair across from Adrian, Caprice slipped onto his lap, then cuddled in and wrapped her arms around his neck. "For now this feels like the place I have to be, if you'll have me."

"I'll have you," he whispered, pulling her into his chest.

With her ear pressed to him, Caprice listened to the steady beat of Adrian's heart for a while. Strong rhythm, perfect. Nothing to reflect stress. Nothing to reflect the way it surely must be breaking.

Over the next minutes she snuggled in deeper, kicking off her shoes and pulling her legs up, tucking herself into Adrian until they breathed the same pattern, moved the same movements. Felt like they were the same person.

Quietly, he stroked her hair, causing the flesh down her back to tingle with the sweet anticipation of more. But they couldn't. Not under these circumstances. He ran his fingers through her hair, trailed them down to her neck, then tracked a delicate line around to her jaw—the most exquisite sensation she'd ever felt in her life.

Caprice shivered, sucking in her breath. How she wanted this man. Wanted more than his fingers tracing a path on her. Wanted everything. Turning, she'd barely moved her cheek away from his chest when he lowered his head and found her lips. The need between them was strong. The kisses weren't the gentle kisses of earlier, but raw, desperate. Urgent. Kisses she needed in a way she'd vowed she would never need again in her life.

But she needed this, needed Adrian. And it wasn't going to be gentle or prolonged. The harder his lips pressed and the more his tongue delved, the quicker she squirmed into position, until she had to straddle him, her knees on either side of his hips, the two of them too wild in their desires to budge from the mahogany leather chair to a bed upstairs or a sofa in another room.

"Are you sure?" he asked, already unbuttoning her blouse with such frenzy his practiced fingers were nearly clumsy. He was down to the last button, pulling the blouse hem out of her skirt before she found a voice to answer.

"Yes!" she cried. Her voice was so unusually husky she didn't recognize it.

Yes—that one word was all it took for Adrian to rid her of her blouse completely, tossing it into the dark somewhere. Next came her bra, a pink wisp of a thing that, likewise, disappeared into the dark.

"You have no idea how much I've wanted this," he growled, moving forward for a taste of her breast.

The first sensation of his lips on her nipple caused Caprice to gasp and shudder. This was the first *real* sexual sensation of her life. Nothing had come before this, nothing that mattered, and she wanted it…wanted it so badly she arched her back, thrusting more of herself against him…to his mouth, feeling brazen enough to take if he didn't offer. "I do have an idea how much," she replied in her own, throaty growl, the fire inside now overpowering her.

She could feel his erection pushing into her, feel the hard length of it through his pants, through her panties, and what it was causing in her… With abandon, Caprice wiggled herself into the perfect place and started to rock as Adrian still pleasured himself with her breasts, his tongue darting from one to another, his teeth nibbling, his lips devouring. She couldn't hold back, couldn't put off the release. Biting down on her lip, Caprice let herself go with a quiet moan.

"You're killing me, doing that," Adrian groaned, waiting until she was finished and breathless before he pushed her off him just a little.

"Good," she purred, pushing up enough to finally rid herself of her panties. As she started to pull them down, he shoved her hand away and impatiently grabbed them himself, then shot them like a slingshot, out to the vast, unknown darkness with the rest of her clothes. "But if you want more than this, you're going to have to get naked with me now. I mean, I rather enjoyed the solo act, but now it's time for doubles."

"I thought you'd never ask," he said, his voice raspy as he started to push her off his lap. But she stopped him, and pulled his T-shirt off, none too easily. Then she slid down him until she was on her knees on the floor before him, fumbling with his zipper, pulling his jeans off, throwing them out to join her clothes.

Even though the room was dark, cast into golden shadows from the single light, Caprice gasped when his body was fully revealed to her. Firm, well muscled. In a doctor's mind, perfect. In a lover's mind, beyond gorgeous.

And he was ready for her. Stretched out in his chair, naked, erect, he simply watched her as she stood to remove her skirt, the very last piece of clothing between the two of them.

When Caprice was fully naked, she stood boldly in front of Adrian for a moment to let him look, then, when she couldn't stand it any longer, she climbed back into his lap, but this time not to be cozy. She settled right into the spot she had craved more than she'd craved anything sexually in her life and looked down at Adrian as she arched straight up, lowering herself onto him. "It's personal," she whispered, as they started to rock together.

"Always knew it was," he replied, melding into the rhythm at first, then finally dominating it. "Always knew it was," he gasped, as they climaxed urgently, passionately, together.

"What time is it?" Adrian muttered, turning over to look at his alarm clock. At first it surprised him to find Caprice there next to him, but then he remembered. They'd made love together, showered together, made love and showered together again. Then they'd finally gone to bed together...to sleep. And it was now two in the morning and they'd had...one hour?

The phone rang again, reminding him why he'd awakened.

"I'll get it," Caprice mumbled, automatically turning over to search for the phone on the nightstand. Then, like Adrian, she remembered where she was, and her first instinct was to yank the bed sheet up over her naked breasts.

He smiled at the reaction as he picked up the phone. "Adrian McCallan," he said, looking down to find that she had all the sheet and he was lying there totally naked. Not that he minded being totally naked that way with Caprice, but it was odd how natural it seemed.

Caprice rolled back over and snuggled into him, her fingers starting to trace a path from his chest down as the caller on the other end tried to say something Adrian wasn't understanding. "Who is this?" he asked, as her fingers slipped from his chest to his abdomen, then started a journey even farther.

When she reached his erection he grabbed her hand and held it in place, then said into the phone, "Tell me that again."

Seconds later, he repeated an address, then said, "I'll be there in fifteen minutes. Don't let her leave. Do you hear me? Do not let her leave!"

By the time he'd hung up Caprice had already rolled away from him to the edge of the bed. "They've found her again?" she asked.

Adrian was out of bed, on his way to the closet. "Another motel. She checked in a little while ago. The investigator had left a description there and they called him. Sylvie's there right now with Sean." He grabbed out a pair of jeans, then turned around. "Come with me, Caprice."

"Are you sure?" she asked, clutching the sheet around her.

"I'm sure," he said. "More than I've been sure about anything in a long time."

Paul was seated behind the steering-wheel of his car, watching the motel though binoculars with a night scope. "They haven't gone out the front door, but I don't know if there's a window or anything out back. Didn't have time to look around after I got the call."

"But she's been here only an hour?" Adrian asked, hunching down to talk to Paul through the car window.

He shrugged. "According to the night manager. But what worries me is that if she paid him more money to alert her that someone was looking for her than I did to be told she was here, there's no telling about the time frame. She could be running us around again."

"And having a good time doing it," Ben added.

"I say we just go to the door," Adrian said. "We might be lucky." He turned back to Caprice, who was standing outside the car on the sidewalk. "I'll be right back," he said, then the three of them were off.

They were parked well away from the streetlight, but the three forms moving into the dark street were visible in the street-light on the opposite side of the road, and they were imposing and large. Much larger in shadow than in real life. She only hoped that if Sylvie was inside, she wasn't looking out the window right now because if there was a way for her to run away, she would.

She doubted Adrian could face that again.

Caprice drew in a deep breath, waiting, watching, and as Adrian and the others entered the motel parking lot, she noticed a figure running across the street on the other side of the building—a side the men couldn't see from their vantage point! It was a large figure in the shadows, dragging with it…a smaller shadow.

"Sylvie," she whispered to herself, instantly aware that if she shouted to Adrian to warn him, Sylvie might hear, and Adrian probably wouldn't. Even if she used the cellphone, he still wasn't close enough to stop Sylvie from getting on the bus that was stopping half a block away.

Instinct took over. A mother's instinct.

Caprice took off running down the street, her feet hitting the pavement as hard and fast as she'd ever run, and with every step keeping her eyes on the figure ahead of her, watching the figure pull the tinier figure up the bus steps. They were getting away! She couldn't let that happen.

Picking up a pace she hadn't thought she had, she got within sight of the bus and started waving to the driver, trying to hail him, get him to wait for her. Her lungs burned, she could barely get the air dragged into them. But she was closer…getting closer… "Wait," she screamed, even though she knew the driver wouldn't hear her. But she was in his headlights. He could see her running, see her waving. And she was so close.

Then she heard it—the hydraulic noise of shutting doors. "No!" she screamed. "I need to get on!"

Almost there. Just a few more steps. She pumped every last ounce into the last lunge and reached the side of the bus just as the door snapped shut. But she banged on it. With both hands. Frantically. "Open it, please," she called too winded to find much volume. "Please, just let me on."

Suddenly the doors parted, and before they were fully open Caprice wedged herself through them and up the three steep steps, practically falling into the driver's lap before she was able to stop.

The driver, who wasn't wearing a friendly look, simply pointed to the box for the fare, then pulled off. Caprice grabbed a handful of change from her pocket—she didn't know how much—dumped it in the box, then strolled down the aisle amid a few sleepers, a couple of drunks, prostitutes, and finally to the bedraggled woman who was clutching the cutest little red-headed boy Caprice had ever seen.

Still trying to catch her breath, Caprice was careful not to make eye contact with Sylvie as she took her place two seats behind her and punched in the number connecting her to Adrian's cellphone.

When he answered, she mustered a faint whisper. "Got him. We're on the bus." After that, she sat back and waited until the next bus stop, when, at the curb, Adrian, Ben and Paul got on.

"Daddy!" Sean squealed right off, jumping up and running into his father's arms.

As he did that, Sylvie slipped out the back door. And Caprice stayed in her seat, crying. Adrian and Sean were back together and for now that's all that mattered.

Six months later, Costa Rica

Adrian kicked off his shoes and plopped down on the blanket next to Caprice. "It's good to be back," he said, his eye on the edge of the jungle where the children were trying to entice a spider monkey out of a tree.

"I can't believe it's finally over," Caprice said. "And it's good to have you back. I've missed you." She scooted over to him, slipping her hand into his. "Tell me what happened at the hearing."

"Nothing. Sylvie didn't show up. After we told the judge what she'd done, he granted me full custody. I can allow her supervised visits if she wants them, and if I want her to have them, but after her attorney told her she was lucky I wasn't pressing charges for taking Sean against the court's first agreement, she simply vanished. Somehow I don't think she'll be coming back any time soon. So, what's been going on here?"

"Elena came thorough her surgery beautifully, and she's ready to start her orthodontia. Grant was here for about a week then he got called back to Hawaii for an emergency, so I've been working longer hours."

"And just when I wanted some time alone with you. Do you know how long it's been?" he asked, just as Isabella grabbed the cap off Sean's head and started to run toward the jungle with it. "Stop right there, young lady," he called. "You know the boundaries."

"Too long," Caprice said. Truthfully, the past six months had been hectic, spent together mostly on the phone. She'd gone home to California for a while and had been back to Costa Rica for another month prior to this trip. Then she and Isabella had taken two long weekends in Miami with Adrian and Sean. Adrian and Sean had found time for one weekend in California. But there hadn't been much time for Adrian and Caprice alone other than a few stolen moments and the hours when the kiddies slept. Hours when they'd purposely remained very circumspect. Until later, Caprice hoped.

"But if you're interested, I have a new medical team in now, Josefina has agreed to watch both of the children for a couple of days, and I know a nice little guest house on a beautiful beach where you can swim in the shadows. White sands, practically deserted. Not a very long drive from here. In fact, we can still make it during daylight if we get started soon," Caprice said. To tempt him, she pulled a very skimpy swimsuit from her bag, gave him a quick peek, then tucked it away, glad that even in the Costa Rican rainy season, as they were in now, there was a lot of good beach weather to be had.

"Sounds *and looks* personal to me, Dr Bonaventura," he said, arching a suggestive eyebrow.

"I intend it to make it very personal, Dr McCallan."

Caught between taking a peek at the swimsuit and watching Sean tease Isabella, the children's tiff won out for the moment. "Sean, give that doll back to Isabella!" Adrian shouted, then bent toward Caprice and gave her a quick kiss. "The sooner the better on getting personal."

Caprice frowned. "Are you sure about us, Adrian? I mean, now that we've settled back into our normal lives, is this what you really want? Some things will never change with me. You know that."

"And maybe someday I can help you to quit blaming yourself for your sister's death. I want to do that, Caprice. It's a tough journey you shouldn't have to take alone, and I want to take it with you."

"I want you there, Adrian. But it scares me."

"And the thought of me not being with you scares me, Caprice. We're going to get through it together. Maybe not today or tomorrow, maybe not in a month or a year, but I promise, sweetheart, it will happen. And you're not going through those feelings and guilt alone any more."

"You want me," she whispered, more as a reassurance to herself than as a statement or question. Sometimes she still didn't believe this was happening to her. Couldn't believe how lucky she was to have Adrian in her life, in her heart. And her in his. Yes, there were times when she doubted this was happening to her, when she was scared it would all disappear, but he always knew what to say and what to do to make her feel better. Make her feel safe. Make her feel loved.

"You're all I want," he said. "And once the two of you get settled in with us in Miami, it's going to get a lot easier. I promise, sweetheart. It will be so much easier. Besides, my mother's elated about the prospect of having another child around to care for. Especially a girl. She already loves Isabella, tells people she has a new granddaughter. So tell me, are *you* sure about *us*? About taking *two* men into your lives?"

"You changed my mind in so many ways," she said, leaning her head against his shoulder. "You're not all bastards, you know."

He laughed, then gave her a quick kiss on the forehead. "And you're not *all* issues now that you've mellowed out."

"Mellowed?" she asked, snaking her hand up to twine through his hair. "And how would I have mellowed?"

"Sex does that," he whispered. "Has a way of unwinding us."

"We haven't…not that much."

He laughed. "So just think how mellow and unwound you're going to be once we do *that much*."

"Have I told you how much I love you, Dr McCallan?" she said, positioning herself to kiss him full on the lips.

"Not nearly as much as I've told you how I love you, Dr Bonaventura," Adrian said, positioning himself for that kiss.

He bent his head toward her as she inclined hers toward him, and as their lips were about to brush she jerked away. "Isabella! Don't entice that monkey down out of the tree with your paw-paw. And, Sean, don't give Isabella your paw-paw so she can entice the monkey."

They both laughed as they traded the passionate kiss for a brief one, then jumped up together and ran after the children. It was going to be a good life, Caprice thought, following the man who would be her husband once they returned to Miami. Her cause was the same, and her passion for the work of Operation Smiling Faces as great as ever. But now it was different. She had someone who understood her, who supported her, who shared her passions. Someone who loved her, and loved Isabella. Someone she loved with all her heart. And a little boy she loved now, too.

Yes, it was going to be a very good life.

Medical Romance™

COMING NEXT MONTH
TO MEDICAL ROMANCE SUBSCRIBERS

Visit www.eHarlequin.com for more details

Desert Doctor, Secret Sheikh by **Meredith Webber**
Dr. Jenny Stapleton has devoted herself to those in need around the globe, risking her life but never her heart. Then, in Zaheer, she meets Dr. Kam Rahman. But Kam is not just a doctor—he's a sheikh! Sheikh Kamid Rahman is soon to ascend the throne, and he wants this desert doctor as his queen!

A Single Dad at Heathermere by **Abigail Gordon**
The pretty village of Heathermere is not only a home but also a sanctuary for Jon Emmerson and his young daughter, Abby. Here he can simply focus on being a father and the local doctor, leaving his past far behind—until the day he bumps into childhood friend Dr. Laura Cavendish. Laura is a struggling single parent, too, and before long Jon realizes they are meant to be a family.

The Italian Count's Baby by **Amy Andrews**
Nurse Katya Petrov believes her unborn baby really needs its father. But talented Italian surgeon Count Benedetto, with whom she spent one passionate night, has no idea she is pregnant. Once he finds out, though, it becomes clear that he wants to be a father to his child, and he offers Katya marriage—for the baby's sake! But Katya secretly longs for Ben to one day give her his heart, as she has already given him hers.

The Heart Surgeon's Secret Son by **Janice Lynn**
Nurse Kimberly Brooks has postponed her week-long training session with leading heart surgeon Daniel Travis once already. Even though she feels like running for the hills, she can't put it off any longer. She has to go into surgery and face the man she once loved with all her heart. But, as the week goes on, Kimberly feels the pressure of her renewed feelings for Daniel, and of her untold secret—he is the father of her son.

HMEDCNM0208

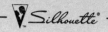

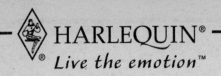

HARLEQUIN®
Live the emotion™

American ROMANCE®

Heart, Home & Happiness

♦ HARLEQUIN®

Blaze™

Red-hot reads.

♦ HARLEQUIN®

E V E R L A S T I N G L O V E™

Every great love has a story to tell™

♦ Harlequin® Historical

Historical Romantic Adventure!

♦ HARLEQUIN®

H A R L E Q U I N R O M A N C E®

From the Heart, For the Heart

♦ HARLEQUIN®

INTRIGUE

Breathtaking Romantic Suspense

Medical Romance™...
love is just a heartbeat away

Next™

**There's the life you planned.
And there's what comes next.**

♦ HARLEQUIN®
Presents~

Seduction and Passion Guaranteed!

♦ HARLEQUIN®
Super Romance®

Exciting, Emotional, Unexpected

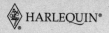

INTRIGUE

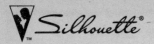

Romantic
SUSPENSE.

**Sparked by Danger,
Fueled by Passion.**

When Tech Sergeant Jacob "Mako" Stone opens
his door to a mysterious woman without a past,
he knows his time off is over. As threats to Dee's
life bring her and Jacob together, she must set
aside her pride and accept the help of the military
hero with too many secrets of his own.

Out of Uniform
by Catherine Mann

Available February wherever you buy books.

Silhouette® Desire

NEW YORK TIMES BESTSELLING AUTHOR

DIANA PALMER

A brand-new Long, Tall Texans novel

IRON COWBOY

Available March 2008
wherever you buy books.